Living with Vampires

By Belinda Topan

Email: info@belindatopan.com.au

characters, and locations are products of the author's imagination.

Book design by Angie Alaya

Artwork Created by Babycado

Twitter: babycado_

Email: babycadochan@gmail.com

Editing Author Services Australia:

Marilyn Boake

Second printing edition 2023

www.belindatopan.com.au

Facebook: www.facebook.com/belindatopan/

Instagram: @belindatopan

Before You Read

Hello!

Thank you so much for picking up my book Living With Vampires. I had a lot of fun writing this novel back in 2019, when I first started writing online. It was a successful little story massing to over 20k reads on Tapas. The slice of life genre influences this novel with certain chapters in the story that are fun, little add ons that tie in between the series parts of the story.

Once you finished the novel, there will be ten extra fun chapters to give in an insight to day-to-day lives and character's thoughts and feelings along with a cut chapter. Not all slice of life moments could be in the main part of the story, but they can be fun extras.

I hope you enjoy Living with Vampires!

- Belinda

Chapters

Blog 1

Date: April 15th
Time: 11:57pm

'Now you'd think living with three other roommates would be difficult, especially when you're the only female living with three males. I'm also the only one who also buys all the food, uses the bathroom, or uses the heating, or does anything that is remotely normal.

Now I know what you're thinking. "You pay for everything? Why don't you just move?" Good question. Given the cost of living, plus paying rent, living anywhere on your own is hella expensive. Hence why it's way cheaper to room with strangers. Or at least semi-sane strangers, who you believe won't kill you in your sleep. Besides, we made an exclusive agreement.

I sho-'

I jump in my seat. The intense yelling interrupted me from my monologue. I groaned into my hands at the miss typed word.

With a sharp push on my black office chair, shuffling into my favourite dragon slippers. Avoiding any chance to feel the cold, dreaded dark oak floorboards. I force myself onto my feet, flipping my onesie's hoodie over my short brown hair.

"Neil, how many times have we told you? Stop bringing dinner home!" I hear a familiar posh British accent echoing through the door.

"Fuck off, I do what I want," a deep voice snaps back. I groan. Introducing my forehead to the door, and a sharp sting blossoms across my nerves. I wait and the apartment falls in silence. Filling my lungs with needed courage, wincing from the cold metal and turn the handle.

The oak door, swollen from humidity, creaks and groans. So much for being discrete.

Staring down the small hallway, in view of the wide open area of the apartment. Three pairs of red eyes, with slit pupils, stare back at me from the open lounge space. Awkwardly standing behind the leather couch, shielding themselves. I notice blonde hair tousled over the couch, followed by the smell of sweet tacky perfume wafting in the air.

Neil's dinner, I assume.

I pity her. Becoming someone's dinner isn't pleasant. You go out, thinking you're going to have a great time, only then to have your life drained from your body and become a bloodless corpse. A cruel way to go.

"Did we ah - wake you?"

I stare at the tanned man to the left of the trio. His curled moustache quivers in anticipation of my answer. He shifts under my stare, moving the few dark brown untamed strands of his hair off his face and slicking them back. The sheen of his hair reflects so much light it could set fire to a small bush.

'*I swear he uses too much product.*'

"No, you didn't. Thank you for asking Nathaniel." He relaxes and straightens his stripe-print jacket over his black buttoned up shirt.

My roommates. The most dysfunctional, chaotic bunch of misfits you will ever meet. Every day is a new argument, and one liner burns. Each one with a conflicting personality, wondering how they haven't killed each other yet.

Nathaniel draws his attention to Neil. The younger vampire continuous to glare at me, baring his slightly bloody fangs. On Neil's right, Brooklyn just stares off into space, scratching his black beard in thought. "Do I ask, or a better question is, do I have to help?" I ask them. Oblivious that I had entered the scene, Brooklyn snaps out of his daze and waves at me.

"Nah, we got this," Brooklyn pitches in, with his distinct American accent. Giving a fanged smile straight after. I sigh in relief.

I direct my attention to Neil; his trademarked cold glower is on me. I flip him off before stepping back into my room. The door moans in protest, and I hear a dull thump on the other side, followed by a muffled groan escaping Niels' mouth. So much for fast reflexes.

"C'mon Neil, let's get this body out of here," I hear Brooklyn call out to him.

"At least you didn't get any blood on the leather or the rug. This couch is expensive," Nathaniel whines. I lean back on the door as I hear the three of them clean the mess outside. The plushes perched on my antique writer's desk stare back at me with their unnerving black eyes, as if their very gaze could take my soul. When I first moved into the room, Nathaniel called the desk a little welcoming gift. Though he was just lazy and didn't want to move it out of the room but now, when he looks at it, I always receive a snarky remark.

"Wasting your money on hideous nick knacks, I see."

He sulks every time he looks at the desk with disdain.

Before the interruption, I stare at the unfinished blog post, running over the paragraph I knew so well in my head. I stare back at my laptop. Patiently, my story waits for my return. Whether it will be five minutes or five years, it will remain. I nod to myself. Sleep can wait.

I scuttle back to my seat, leaving the warm slippers on and rearrange my words.

'I should explain. What I am about to write may sound crazy. Most people will never believe me. That's OK. I need this. Writing is the only thing that is keeping me sane. Allow me to start from the beginning...'

Blog 2

Date: April 20th,
Time: 8:32 am

'It happened three months ago. My foolishness and pure nature believed in the ad's legitimacy. I noticed it in the paper, just sitting in the centre of the page standing out in hideous comic Sans font. That would have been my first clue.'

The scrunched paper shook in my palms. I re-read the article. Words mixed and blurred together as my visions fade in and out, whilst I quiver in the middle of the elevator. Looking back down, my eyes were quick to catch the intense red circle around the article, making it obvious for me to identify it. I knew the article was in the centre of the paper. On impulse, I had to comb every nook and cranny of the page before it took me back to the spot I required. A brief gasp left my mouth as the dull bell rang, signalling the end of my ride. The steel doors opened, and a dark-coloured oak door stared back at me, mocking me, daring me to move closer. I swallow the lump in my throat and forced one foot out on the awful darkened teal carpet. My eyes landed on the ominous stains just a few feet before me. It appeared to be fresh and damp still.

'This was my second clue; you'd think seeing something ambiguous on the carpet would send dread to my brain? It wasn't.'

I stopped in the hall to look back down at the horrid paragraph.

Room Mate Wanted!

Spacious Penthouse apartment in the Melbourne CBD. Luxurious garden balcony, state-of-the-art kitchen (imported from Italy). A small room available for cheap. Sharing with three other flatmates.

- Neil

No last name, nothing, just an address. My gut twists as I am weighed by the dark thoughts filling my head. All with the possibilities of them being a rapist or a serial killer? What choice did I have? It's not like I had anywhere else to go. With a sharp breath, I tiptoed closer to the tired oak door, patches of varnish stripped away with time, exposing the wood to the elements. My hand shook as I reached for the decadent lion's head doorknocker, the ring in its mouth tarnished to a golden yellow, its predatory eyes staring back at me. I drew a ragged breath, desperate to soothe my erratic pulse. The chill from the handle seeped into my palm, and I tapped. One, two, three.

Shuffling resonated from the other side, and the door creaked open. Unnatural red eyes peered back at me through the crack. I swallowed, taking a step back. A fanged smile emerged, and an icy grip grabbed my arm, forcing me inside. I tripped and landed on all fours. My knees hurt as they crashed into the hardwood. I turned on my rear to meet the cruel-looking man looming over me, his eyes filled with an unexplainable hunger.

He seemed human at first glance, but the glow of his red eyes, slit pupils, and fanged smile gave his secret away. Cocking his head to the side, the careless strands of black hair covered his face. Scowling, he raked his fingers through, trying to remove the loose strands aside but failing. His predatory hunger washed away, and an endearing boyish awkwardness shone through. Reminiscent of a young teen getting ready for a date.

"Can't believe it worked," he purred to himself.

"Neil, who is at the door?" A sharp tone cuts across the room.

"Nobody!" Neil shouted, his stare focused on me.

He took one step forward, his black boots screeching against the wooden floor. They echoed with every thump. I clambered backward, my vision never leaving the creature.

My palms pressed into smooth, cold flesh. I let out a shaky breath, tearing my gaze from the creature and looking down to see my hand on top of a foot. My stomach plummeted, and my heart was in my throat.

I saw an immaculate trimmed beard and another pair of red eyes staring at me. Stilling, I begged them to forget me so I could sneak out.

"Nobody, huh?" the unshaven man grinned, and Neil rolled his eyes.

"Keep this between us, and I'll share," Neil compromised, and the bearded man hummed.

"I'm just wondering how this little human ended up on our doorstep," he questioned.

My hand shot up and waved the newspaper centimetres from his face. The shaggy man staggered backward before grasping the paper from my hand and thanking me.

With his eyes locked on mine, the younger of the two looked ready to pounce on me.

"Nathaniel!" The bearded one cried out, somewhat echoing in the vacant spaces of the penthouse.

"Don't call him, Brooklyn!" the young one snarled, baring his fangs.

"Neil just gave our residency away, just so he could get an easy meal!" Brooklyn called out into the void.

Neil charged at him. Their heads just missed the edge of the couch as they tussled on the floor.

I thanked the universe and crawled towards the exit while their scuffle kept them from noticing me.

I stopped. The surrounding noise washed out like the waves in the ocean. In front of me was a nice pair of black leather dress shoes, leading up to a pair of grey slacks, followed by a grey button-up shirt. A tanned skin gentleman crossing his arms blocked my escape. His eyes matched the two behind me. His curled moustache quivered upwards as he smiled.

'I lie if I said I knew what they were. Giving the descriptions I have written, it's pretty easy to tell. But granted, in my panicked state, I didn't care. All I cared about was getting out alive.'

The man with the sun kissed skin intervened and pulled one off the other and ordered everyone to separate in their own seats before dragging me over to one of the two lounges.

"Care to explain yourself, Neil?" the tanned curly-stashed creature asked, standing at the door, his arms crossed over his chest.

Neil kept his arms crossed and nose turned downwards to the floor. His silence spoke louder. His cuts and gashes bled over the furniture as he sat in the armchair like a child. My mouth hangs open, enraptured by how his wounds stitched themselves together. The bearded one lounged on the couch across from me, not a single scratch on him. His lips curled upward, his expression dripping with self-satisfaction, and waited for Neil's answers.

Neil's lips moved in a faint whisper, inaudible to the human ear.

"Sorry, I didn't quite get that," Curly Stache sang.

"I wanted an easy meal," Neil spoke up.

'Why am I dinner?'

He marched over with the newspaper in hand.

"And you think this–," he paused and waved the paper in front of him. "Would be a great idea!" he shouted.

"I didn't think a human would be dumb enough," Neil murmured.

"And then what, Neil? You kill the human, and all's right with the world!" Curly Stache yelled. "You don't think!" he finished with a growl.

He waved the paper in his face again, "Just think, missing person reports, police investigations, our address, telling everyone where she went!" his voice raised with each process, reaching the point of hysterical yelling. We all heard chuckling across the room as the fine-dressed gentleman turned to the scraggy-looking man.

"And what!" he paused, marching to the flannel-wearing, shoeless, bearded creature, "do you think is funny?"

"We still have to kill her," he sniggered.

"Have you not been listening to a word I have been saying?" he yelled.

"She knows what we are or what he was planning to do," the flannel lover pointed to Neil. "What makes you think she wouldn't go to the police?" he explained. Curly Stache straightened up. His head turned to me.

My body stiffened, pleading there was some god to make me disappear.

"Well, my dear, do you know what we are?" he asked me lovingly.

I shook my head.

"God, you humans are dumb." Neil's lips curled back and exposing his large canines. "We're fucking vampires. How dense are you!" he snarls. Curly Stache's mouth dropped open. Flannel lover lost it with laughter. Something in me snapped.

"Oh, I'm sorry, but I was trying to focus on not dying!" I snapped. "If you weren't trying to kill me, I could think about it!" I sarcastically replied.

Flannel lover barked out even louder with laughter, and Curly Stache blinked, his mouth still open.

"I suggest you close your mouth, or you'll catch flies," I muttered, crossing my arms.

Curly Stache closed his mouth and cleared his throat. Straightening his dress shirt and composing himself again. "I see your point, Brooklyn."

Flannel lover calmed down and smiled at Curly Stache. "Well, what will we do with her?"

I stiffened, feeling my tough composure melt away like ice on a hot summer's day, as they all look at me with hungry eyes.

"Wait!" I shouted, raising my hands. "Let's make a deal!"

"What?" they all said in unison.

"A deal. What you said in the ad, is it true?" I asked and pointed to Neil.

"Well–I–may–yeah, I told the truth," Neil stumbled over his words before admitting the truth. Curly Stache directed his attention to Neil, glowering at the fellow vampire.

"See, perfect, you let me stay here for free."

"What!"

"Let me finish," I snapped. "I'll pay for all my food and part of the bills. Just let me stay in the room."

"What do we get out of it?" Curly Stache asked.

"You won't have to worry about the body if you kill me, and if I live with you guys, you have the best chance to monitor me. No loose lips," I smiled at the end of my pitch.

Please say yes.

"I don't see why not," the bearded one shrugged.

"Brooklyn!" the tanned vampire snarled.

“What?” he asked. “I think it’s a pretty good deal,” he grinned, leaning back and resting his head on his hands.

“I protest!” Neil snarled, baring his fangs at the other two.

“Shush child, adults are talking,” Brooklyn snipped back. “Well, Nathaniel,” he darted his eyes back to the vampire in question. “Your choice.”

Nathaniel rubbed his face with both hands, groaning in frustration.

“For the sake of secrecy,” he snarled. “You can stay.”

'Even though I regret thinking of the idea in the first place, I commend myself. My quick thinking just kinda saved my ass.'

Curly Stache led me to the back. There were three doors in the hall, two adjacent and one at the end.

With an eerie creak, it impressed me to see the black curtains still blocking out the natural light, as the sun's rays sneaked through the moth-eaten holes. A thin layer of dust coated the floor, boxes scattered and strewn amongst the room filled with old knick-knacks and antique posters. Racks of clothes from different eras now collected dust and became a lovely food source for moths. The lone notable piece of furniture was the old writer's desk, sitting cozily in the corner.

"Oh dear," Curly Stache murmured. His nose crinkled, eyeing at the room's disarray. "Well, I hope you like it here." He walked away. My heart hammered out of my chest, a horrid lump weighing in my throat, and anxiety holding my stomach, threatening to lose all the contents of my lunch on the floor. I took deep breaths, recounting the last hour in my head, asking if I had made the right choice.

I focus on the box sitting on the old writer's desk, beckoning to come closer.

Stacked inside were vintage comic books, with unscratched covers, yet the colours remained vivid and eye-captivating. Only two, maybe three, had faded away.

"You won't last." I jumped and dropped the comic back into the box. Turning to find Neil leaning on the door frame, his arms crossed over his chest. "Give it a month, and you'll be begging to leave," he said. Neil straightened himself up and walked up to me. "And when you do," he leaned in, close to my ear. "I'll kill you." My heart stuttered, giving my fear away. Neil pulled back and smiled. “Enjoy your stay,” he finished, and grabbed the box behind me.

Goodbye, late night reading.

'So that’s how I met them. Not the most glamorous or most intelligent. Hopefully, I am still alive by the time I have a chance to write more of these.'

Blog 3

Date: April 22nd
Time: 9:30 pm

'I'm alive! I am actually alive, and I am questioning my sanity. Ninety percent of you don't believe me, which is fine, but I am happy to answer the most asked question here.

What are the biggest issues when you live with three vampires?

Some of you would answer, blood packs in the fridge, or a dismembered body in the living space, (bit extreme). It irked me initially, but I am thankful that I am not on the menu.'

Standing on the tips of my toes, reaching for the last button. The edge of my finger just pressed into it. The steel doors opened and people rushed to escape the confined space. Those who stayed spread like the red sea as I stepped in.

I got it. I smelled.

The door cries open and the delicious aroma of roast potatoes and seared meat. My mouth watered and my stomach grumbled. Neil was in the middle of a heated make-out session with a half-naked man, unaware of my presence. Last but not least, the dining table. Scattered cutlery and two plates, with the heavy coat of gravy and bloody residue from the meat. Half-filled wine glasses sat close together, one white, the other red.

I took a deep breath and slammed the door shut. Both men jumped apart, staring at me like frightened deer. The shirtless stranger gobsmacked, eyes popping out, mouth slack, looking like a surprised goldfish. Neil's eyes, no longer the vibrant red, now a dulled grey, and filled with scorched hatred.

Poor bastard.

"Oh shit," the goldfish muttered. "You fucking lied to me." He shouted, pointing to me.

Neil's head snapped back at him. "What?!"

"You used my fucking food, you fucktard!" I screamed back.

"What?" the goldfish bellowed.

"Why the hell did you assume she was my girlfriend?" Neil snapped at him, ignoring what I said. The goldfish looked between us, trying to make sense of the situation.

“You selfish dick, I hope you choke,” I yelled at him, stomping into the bathroom.

I heard a deep rumble coming from Neil, and the goldfish screamed. I slammed the white door shut, hearing his muffled cries through the wood. He begged for Neil to stop, but I knew it all fell on deaf ears. I slid down the door, my butt reaching the white tiles.

'Vampires don't care for human life. There are rare cases, but it's far more complicated. I haven't even scratched the surface of how this supernatural world works.

If I stepped in and tried to get between Neil and his meal. I would be dead as well. That is the reason one. Reason two is I 'm getting used to the killing or starting to no longer care. It's a fine line, and I don't know which is which.

More on the annoying things list is; stealing my food just so they could get laid or feed.

Another one is when they criticise your taste in clothing.'

Nathaniel's sharp gasp breaks the silence. "Good lord Valeria!"

"What?" I stopped in my tracks and turned to the tanned vampire. Nathaniel sat in his armchair with a cup of tea on the coffee table and newspaper in hand.

"All black? Are you going to a funeral?" he asked me.

"Yes, a funeral for my happiness," I sarcastically replied. Nathaniel scrunched his nose up.

"No, no, no, this will not do," he dismissed. Instead of folding the paper nice and neat, he threw it down on the coffee table, almost hitting his tea. He shook his head and rose from his seat. "This will not work," he mumbled. Shaking his index finger, he stormed off to the spiral staircase. The sound of fine leather and metal colliding together as he stepped on each metal platform. He returned with his wallet in hand and an elegant trench coat on.

"We need to get you proper clothes," he waved his hand at me.

"My clothes are fine!" I defended, but he shook his head.

"No!" A gust of air blew past me, and Nathaniel was already at the open door. "Not in that rabble you aren't," he argued, and walked out before I could respond.

What just happened?

"I would move it if I were you," I heard Brooklyn call out from the balcony, pruning shears in hand.

'The clothes are nice, but I have no use for them. Way too fancy for my liking and girly. Nathaniel is old school. He is sometimes nice, but too much.'

"Man, I am so excited," Brooklyn giggled, swinging the fridge door open and grabbing blood pouches and a can of coke for me. "A movie night with just the three of us." He set down all the items on the bench and opened the microwave, retrieving the bag of popcorn. “Why didn’t I come up with this idea sooner?” Brooklyn wondered aloud, as he searched the cabinets for a bowl.

“Maybe because we all hate each other, and we’re only doing this because some insecure little human wants to recreate her childhood before it became broken,” Neil gave a snarky reply, followed by a cruel smile.

Don’t bite. Just ignore it.

“Fuck you.”

I didn’t ignore it.

A cackle erupted from Neil before returning to his phone. Brooklyn was halfway in the corner cupboard, digging through the assortment of bowls and containers.

“You okay, Brooklyn?” I asked.

"Yeah, I'm good. Just searching for a bowl." I heard a loud clang inside.

"Why do you guys have so much? You don't even eat," I asked them.

"Nathaniel just likes to collect these," I heard Brooklyn's muffled reply.

"It's so we can 'appear' more human," Neil quoted.

"Ah-hah!" Brooklyn's hand appeared above the black granite counter, with a large steel bowl in hand.

"That or Nathaniel is a closeted hoarder," I added.

"What-movie-are-we-watching?" Brooklyn huffed as he climbed to his feet, using the countertop to take all his weight.

"Wanna watch Men in Leggins?" I asked, and Brooklyn's face lit up.

"Ooo, I haven't seen that in ages," he beamed. "Last time I saw it was when it came to the theatre," he gloated and poured the popcorn into the bowl.

Neil hopped off the barstool. "Whelp, I hope you have a good time," he said, heading to his room.

Brooklyn sped in front of Neil's bedroom door, with his arms crossed and fangs bared, blocking Neil's attempt to escape.

'Neil doesn't enjoy socialising, no matter who it is. Brooklyn has forced Neil to go through many social situations. It's called "Operation: Get Neil to open up about his feelings and enjoy having friends." While the title may need improvement, Brooklyn's heart is in the right place.'

I watched the projector screen ascend down from the ceiling, just missing the seats of the adjacent couch. Brooklyn wrestled with cables and wires, scratching his beard in contemplation, unsure how the machine worked. Neil sat on the armchair furthest away from us, my laptop in his lap, keeping it close to him as if his life depended on it.

After ten minutes of Brooklyn fiddling, the screen came to life. Neil moved the mouse cursor to the movies and double-clicked. He sifted through the files, glancing at me every so often. The mouse cursor landed on a gay romance movie, and Neil raised his eyebrow at me and smirked.

Brooklyn plopped himself down, popcorn bowl in hand and blood packs in the other. He handed me the popcorn and threw one blood pack to Neil. Neil caught the bag with one hand and kept scrolling through the list. He stopped at the folders of all the old anime about a children's card game.

"You're such a dork," Neil murmured and kept scrolling. Neil finally stopped and clicked on the film.

Brooklyn's face lit up, and it was the biggest grin you could see from space.

'There is another issue I face. Well, more like we face. It starts with an over dramatic entrance.'

We made it as far as the buildings burning and everyone yelling. The door slammed open, and Nathaniel slowly turned pale. His eyes darted around the apartment, each inhale sharper and deeper than the last, and he slowly removes his hand from the door. He became more rigid with each step, only stopping at the kitchen, glancing at the clothes strewn across the lounge, his head turning to the dirty dishes and plates on the counter, plastic containers pulled out from the cupboard, the microwave door left open, dirty footprints on the timber floor, and a few pieces of popcorn at Neil's feet.

"Everyone out!" Nathaniel snapped.

"What!" we all shouted in unison.

"Members of the King's coven are coming here, and I need this place spotless!" he shouted, frenzied around the penthouse and picking up clothes Brooklyn left behind.

"And that means you three are out!" he shouted.

"That's not fair!" I yelled. Nathaniel flashed before me, his vibrant red eyes flaring with fury.

"You little miss," he hissed. "Should be thankful that you are alive. Living here because of my good graces!" I nodded as if my neck was stiff, swallowing my rage down, and said nothing. Removing myself from the couch with the popcorn bowl in hand, I walked over to Neil.

"May I please have my laptop back?" I asked in a quiet voice. Neil didn't answer. He just closed the lid and passed it to me. I felt my heart rip as I threw out the popcorn. "I'll find a place to stay for the night," I muttered, passing Nathaniel. Entering my room, I threw my laptop into its bag and proceeded to grab clothes for the night.

"That was uncalled for," I heard Brooklyn defend me.

A sad smile crept upon my lips. It was a small sign of hope.

'Nathaniel's goal in life is to be in the higher circles. I'm thankful Brooklyn and Neil are not like that. The night wasn't all bad, though. Brooklyn stole Nathaniel's credit card and rented the most expensive hotel for the night. When I get a chance, I'll write about what happened another time. Besides, wait till you read what happens next!'

Blog 4

Date: 3rd of May
Time: 10:45am

'It's been a while. A lot of you have been asking about any additional problems and I have more to tell. Starting off with the biggest pain in my ass since arriving at the apartment.'

"I don't see why you have to come with me," I whined, pushing my shopping trolley through each aisle, searching each item with careful consideration, desperate to save a few cents.

"I have my reasons," Neil replied, keeping his arms crossed as he watched me shop.

Neil scrunched his nose in disgust as I looked through the frozen food section. He stood there in the cold air, reading through the ingredients and nutritional information, unbothered by the chill, equally shocked and disgusted by what he saw.

Neil disregarded the curious gazes from the other customers. “Do you realise what you humans have been eating!?” he shouted across the aisle. I froze, hearing him from far behind me. People stared at me, all waiting for a response, a scene, something.

I gripped the handle of the trolley and took a deep breath, looking at the ground beneath and wishing it would open up.

Spinning around. Neil still held the coloured packaged food in his hand, his brow raised with anticipation.

I grabbed his arm, pulling him away from the freezer section, and raced out of view to another aisle, relieved to see not a soul in sight.

"God, you're irritating," I murmured.

'Having a vampire shop with you is interesting, but annoying at the same time.'

"Please don't do that again," I gritted, rubbing my temples.

"It was just a simple question," he shrugged, crossing his arms, noting the contents in the trolley, cocking his head to the side.

"You don't just yell out humans. You say my name and then complain to me." Neil just stared at the trolley, eyes glassy and unresponsive, a blank canvas.

"Do you know what? Yell it out. Then hopefully, a slayer kills you, or you get dragged off to a medical ward. That way, I can shop in peace."

Neil's brows knit together.

"Why do you only have bread, milk, and frozen vegetables?" he asked.

"Were you even listening?"

"No." he replied. "I was trying to figure out why you have so little in there," he explained, looking back at the trolley.

"Oh well, that's simple," I began, sarcasm dripped from my voice. "Since I study full time and have a part-time job that doesn't want to pay someone who is in their early twenties and prefers to pay young fifteen-year-old kids, so they give most of the hours to them. And therefore, whatever money I have scrounged up together, I can buy myself decent food, but that only happens once in a blue moon. And I was so looking forward to that steak because it's a rare occasion that I get some meat, period. Do you know how expensive it is these days? I'm lucky that I don't pay rent, but with the shit hours I get weekly, most of what I get goes to the bills for my side of the portion!" I yelled at him.

"I was turned in the seventies. A lot has changed in the last forty years."

'According to Nathaniel and Brooklyn, they found Neil in an alley in the early eighties. He never spoke about his turning, how old he is, his life–nothing. We only know this version of Neil. His past shrouded in mystery.'

"I'm surprised. Things were so cheap back then, none of this imported shit," he hummed. Neil grasped the handle of the trolley, turned it around with one hand, and headed back to the freezer section.

"Uh, what are you doing?" I asked him, catching up with the swift vampire.

"Buying your food. You said it was expensive."

I kept my mouth shut. It's not that I didn't mind or hate the idea. The air left my lungs and gawk at the young vampire. "Just consider it as a thank you."

'It's the first time Neil did something nice for me. I don't understand what I did, but maybe it was because I didn't bother warning his human meal about the danger he was in? But hey, you never know.'

Blog 5

6th of May
Time: 1:54Pm

'Ah yes, those stories about vampires having supernatural abilities. They're true. Hypersensitive nose, hypersensitive big ears—who enjoy ruining my evenings.'

The bodies on the crowded dance floor bounced in sync with the vibration of the rocking beat bouncing off the walls. In the main bar area, people stacked on top of each other, their smells merging into an undecipherable scent, some combination of beer, whiskey, cigarettes, and pot. The designated smoking area was a thick haze of blue, tendrils of smoke curled upwards as if spirits were rising from the floor. Each breath I took left a gritty ash taste on my tongue. The people of Melbourne smoked like chimneys! Then there were those pinned to the brick outer walls of the bar, hiding away from the judging gazes of patrons.

Who cleaned the floor? Did they even use soap?

Individuals felt more at ease leaning against the walls, instead of approaching the stage.

Moving closer to the bar, I struggled to hear the music, and conversations lost in the noise, the void filled with chattering voices. The walls contained a diverse array of faces and personalities, all brought together in one location.

I waited to order a drink but jumped as icy hands slapped my shoulders. I let out a yelp, spinning to face the perpetrator.

"So, this is the place you were talking about," Neil said.

"Neil!" I yelled, drawing attention to ourselves. Everyone around us was watching, some glaring toward his direction, others putting their drinks down, ready to step between us.

Neil continued to wear his grin and bowed down dramatically. I heard some girls giggle, whispering to each other. The vampire shot them a glare, eyes boring into them. It was only a matter of time before he struck. These girls had signed their death warrants.

I fought the crowd to a quiet corner, the vampire's shirt in my hand.

"What are you doing here?" I asked through clenched teeth.

"Apparently there's a... what do you call him? Senpai? Whatever that means will be here, and you're incredibly fond of him," Neil answered. The fiery flames of rage extinguished, and dread only then pooled within my stomach. "Valeria, I never pictured you as a stalker or a yandere–did I pronounce that right?" he asked himself, looking at the ceiling.

"It's not like that," I said.

"Oh, really? I swear, I heard you lying on the living room floor, explaining how perfect he is." Heat rushed to my cheeks. It so was hot it could burn my face off. "Or smoothly talk to him and about his works like senpai is a different person," he mocked.

"I swear to god," I snarled.

The vampire laughed hard and put his stiff arm around me.

“Oh, lighten up. I would do nothing,” Neil assured. “It’s more fun to watch you squirm,” he purred. Neil’s face was close to my neck, his icy breath tickled my skin, raising the hairs on the back of my neck. He inhaled deeply and sighed.

“What would I do to tear into that neck of yours?” he growled.

I clenched my fists together and pushed the vampire off me. Our gazes bow to one another, standing our ground.

“You are the most insufferable creature I have ever met. For once in your life, could you stop being a selfish dick?” He opened his mouth, but I cut him off before he could answer. “You act like the fucking universe owes you–news flash, it doesn’t! Now let me enjoy my night and piss off!”

I stormed off, slamming into his shoulder for good measure.

Fresh air was what I needed. I needed something; I needed a drink. This was a bad idea.

So absorbed in my thoughts, I was stuck in the middle of the cluster of people trying to reach the outside bar. Not only was it the outdoor bar, but it was also the smoking area.

Fuck.

I was caught in a riptide in an ocean of people, forced to walk deeper into the crowd but unable to change direction. I ran into a large-breasted woman who was also swimming against the current of the crowd, trying to reach the bar while I tried to escape. She apologised with a smile.

"I've hit so many people with these," she yelled, referring to her breasts. I gave a nervous laugh, unsure how to react altogether. "Who are you here to see?"

I answered her question as loud as possible. Together with so many people and the volume of voices crammed in, it made it nearly impossible to hear.

"Cool!" she responded. "I used to fuck the lyricist."

'Weird to put that in. It felt like she needed to confide in someone, and I was the chosen one. I seem to emit an aura that makes people feel at ease enough to share intimate details with. Why?'

Freedom, escape, fresh air. Removed from the throngs of people, I retreated to a quiet corner, waiting for the main event to begin.

A glass of Baileys came into view, covering my phone screen. My vision shifted to the pale face and ruffled black hair of Neil. He avoided eye contact and kept a stone composure.

"I didn't poison it," he insisted. "Consider it a peace offering," Neil added with clenched jaws. Time seemed to slow between us, and the sound of a hundred individuals faded away as if Neil and I were the sole occupants of the venue.

"You're not one to apologise," I remarked.

"Do you want the drink or not?" he snapped. I smiled, carefully grasping the drink out of his hand. My cheeks filled with a warm flush for the second time this evening. Our fingers lightly brushed against each other, and Neil flinched away, flexing his hand where our fingers touched. He straightened his shirt and monitored the surrounding crowd. His tough-guy act struggled to stay intact.

"You're still an ass, though," I snickered with a smile.

"I know."

'It was a good night overall. I got to see senpai, and we briefly spoke. I couldn't help but notice Neil staring him down. It seems like he was jealous. I could be wrong. I am just jumping to conclusions. When walking back together, I noticed how jumpy the vampire was, always looking over his shoulder, and rounding the corners first and sniffing the air like a dog on drug patrol. What is he worried about?’

Blog 6

Date: May 20th
Time: 5 PM

'Just want to say thanks to all readers. It makes me happy to know someone out there is crazy enough to read my blogs. I feel a little less insane.'

Blank.

I stared at my computer screen, watching the dash blink over and over, as if tapping its foot, waiting for me to continue to write something.

Don't go on the internet, don't go on the internet.

The time on the corner of the screen taunted me, telling me it was midday, but I knew deep down, it was one in the afternoon.

Curse your daylight savings.

I sighed, throwing my head in my hands, and groaned. I felt a wave of heavy guilt rest upon my shoulders as my words meld themselves together.

My eyes lingered on the city view from the balcony window, marvelling at the tall structures around us and felt the cool wind blowing through the gap of the glass door. Brooklyn's plants rustled in the wind. I saw the bearded vampire tending to the vegetable garden. Vegetables? From a Vampire? He mentioned Neil's name and proceeded with incoherent mumbling when I asked.

I watched him water the array of plants; broccoli, cauliflower, eggplant, zucchini, potatoes. He hummed a tune that I was unfamiliar with, tapping his shoeless feet, splashing in the puddles from the water that had escaped from the pots.

I snorted at the sight. Nathaniel would flip if Brooklyn walked inside with wet feet. The longest I've seen Brooklyn inside lasted five hours, which was during a storm. Nathaniel had to chain him up just so he wouldn't run out in the rain. Not out of any genuine concern for Brooklyn, it was just Nathaniel's way to make sure inside didn't get wet.

The door slid open, and Brooklyn entered, humming a tune, wet puddles trailing behind as he made his way to the kitchen. Reaching for the fridge door, he grabbed a blood packet out. I smiled and returned to my screen as inspiration sparked, lighting a fire in my chest.

"You know, I've noticed how calm Neil seems to be around you," Brooklyn snapped me from my thoughts. I looked up and saw him pour the packet into a mug. "More pleasant to be around," he added. "Haven't seen him bring anyone home in the last month. Which is a record, mind you," Brooklyn continued. The microwave sounded the alarm; Brooklyn's warm snack was ready to be devoured. "Though, I admit, it's good to have you around. Nathaniel has also loosened up." Brooklyn threw his head back, chugging the contents and heaving a heavy sigh of delight.

"Well, you haven't killed me yet, so I must do something right." I said with a chuckle, and Brooklyn snorted, rinsing the mug out with water.

“We were going to.” He shrugged, placing the mug on the drying rack and returning to the balcony, nodding his head to me, asking me to follow him.

I trailed behind, standing near the potted fruit trees, noting the labels for each pot. Blueberry bushes, a skew of fig and lemon trees, a blackberry vine, and apple trees. The wind picked up, and I shivered, feeling the cool breeze dance along my skin. Thoughts of long, warm sunny days and thick humid air caused my heart to ache.

Brooklyn grasped the branch cutters and trimmed the dead branches off the fig trees. “If Neil wasn’t so consumed with the hunt, and Nathaniel focused on gaining a higher status. We would have ended your life within the first week,” he explained.

Their casual mentions of murder, juxtaposed with their calm demeanours, always left me unsettled.

Brooklyn turned to me with a smile.

"And why didn't you?" I asked, crossing my arms.

"I enjoy your company. A rare occurrence for humans to accomplish, but it is possible," Brooklyn laughed to himself and went back to trimming. "Besides, I feel like the universe brought you here. No 'ordinary' human is foolish to fall for Neil's ad," Brooklyn emphasised ordinary and laughed harder than before.

I struggled to resist smiling myself, his laughter infectious, and I felt at ease with this information. A warmth spread within, soothing away the earlier unease.

'The universe, huh? Is there some divine intervention, or a path I follow? Was that ad made for me, the foolish human, to end up living with these vampires? This universe is odd.'

A comfortable silence left us both, staring at the city skyline, and the soothing breeze rustling the leaves.

The familiarity, the comfort; it was as if I had been here forever.

Blog 7

Date: May 21st
Time: 6:54PM

'As much as I appreciate Nathaniel's goals in life. I really appreciate if he told me his plans ahead of time. I would have avoided coming home sooner.'

Brooklyn opened the door for me as he held the more substantial bag of groceries.

"Thank you for coming with me, Brooklyn," I said, rushing through the threshold. The plastic handles dug deep into my fingers, turning them a shade of purple. I dropped the bags on the white tiles, hearing them fall with a heavy thud. I flex, feeling the blood rush back to the tips.

Ow!

Nathaniel drenched in blood. His slack jaw, unruly hair, and eyes, glistening with unshed tears, screaming with silent grief. Two unknown vampires stood in the living room before me. My heart plummeted into the pit of my stomach, sending chills down my spine as my hairs stood on end.

Dread gripped my throat, tightening its hold and freezing my feet in place. All my thoughts screaming at me to get out of here. I felt Brooklyn's hand slap my shoulder, snapping me out of my daze. He gave Nathaniel and his guests a death glare.

"Our apologies. We did not know you were all here," Brooklyn said.

"Yes, this is a surprise," Nathaniel hissed, putting the empty mugs down. He cleared his throat and fixed his hair, pretending that he had just not spilled blood all over him.

"Brooklyn, Valeria, this is some associates from the King coven, from the other worlds. Bellamy and Jayson," Nathaniel introduced.

Other Worlds?

The vampire with wavy hair grasped my hand, bringing me back to the present.

"Bonjour mon chérie," the vampire greeted and kissed the back of my hand.

I stiffened when his lips came into contact. I looked past Bellamy's long brown locks and noticed Neil's bedroom door was still closed.

Still asleep.

My attention turned back to Brooklyn, seeing him pinned to the wall by Jayson. Brooklyn snarled, baring his fangs at the smaller male.

"If you lay a finger on her," Brooklyn threatened.

"Don't bother, we're much stronger than you," the little one chuffed.

"Nathaniel, how thoughtful of you." I turned my head back, feeling my heart ram out of my chest, my throat tightening. Where a charming smile once presented itself, now laid a grinning Cheshire cat, showing off his pearly white canines.

The adrenaline pumped through my veins, all signs screamed to run, but I stood solid. Frozen, as if ice had formed around my feet and I couldn't move.

"Bellamy," Nathaniel warned. He crouched, ready to pounce on his esteemed guest. I felt my jaw go slack, watching the eldest bat for my defence. He was willing to throw his social goals out the window just for my protection.

"Oh?" Bellamy cooed. "Is this one not on the menu?" the vampire's smile became feral. His hand caressed my cheek and sharpened nails danced along my flesh, causing my skin to bristle with goosebumps. "We were just going to have some fun. Weren't we, my dear?" he nicked my cheek, and I felt the small warmth of blood roll down my face. Bellamy leaned in, his icy breath assaulting my face.

I reacted in the only way I knew how. Clenching my free hand and with all the force I could muster, my fist came into contact with his cold cheek. I grimaced, feeling like I just punched a block of concrete.

He pulled back, stunned that I struck a blow on him.

"You're the second one to do that," he snarled, gripping my hand tighter.

"If I were you, I'd let go." Bellamy froze. A hand on his left shoulder, nails morphing into claws, they dug deeper into his flesh. Blood oozed out and stained his white shirt. Bellamy did as he was told and let go of my hand.

I looked behind him and noticed the door wide open and a pissed off Neil, holding Bellamy in his grasp. Bellamy sighed and laughed. He's a psychopath.

"I was wondering when you would come out. It's good to see you, old friend," Bellamy mused and continued to laugh. "You are a hard one to find," he giggled.

"Get the fuck out of my home," Neil hissed, digging his claws deeper. Bellamy grimaced a little, but kept smiling.

"All right, all right, we'll leave," he raised his hand in defence. "It is a pleasure to meet you all. Jayson, let's go."

Jayson released Brooklyn, and the bearded male was ready to charge at Jayson.

"Don't," Nathaniel hissed at Brooklyn, and he did as he was told.

"I'll be keeping in touch, Nathaniel. Expect an invitation in the mail," Bellamy waved at him, passing both Brooklyn and me.

The door closed and echoed through the quiet apartment. We all stood frozen, as if the ice at my feet had cast a spell over the entire room. We all exchanged glances, the weight of unspoken words pressing down on us.

Neil was the first to break the ice and move closer to me. He wiped the blood away with his thumb and rubbed it on his clothes. Neil inspected my face, his cold eyes warm as they looked at every detail of my skin. A shadow of melancholy flickered across Neil's eyes for a second.

"Never let him in our house again," he whispered, eyes still staring into mine.

Neil turned away and sulked back into his bedroom, closing the door as if made of fragile glass and leaving the three of us in a state of shock.

"Whatever is in the invitation, decline it," Brooklyn muttered.

Blog 8

Date: May 22nd
Time: 12:30PM

'Why haven't I seen much of Nathaniel in your writing?' or 'Why don't you write about him more often?' You all ask. Simple answer. With my schedule and whatever Nathaniel does. I don't see him as much as I see Brooklyn or Neil, but I can write some small instances.'

"Nathaniel!" I yelled, slamming my fist upon the wooden oak door. "You've been in there for two hours."

Hopping from one leg to another, the urge intensifying with each passing second. It was the same horrid feeling when you dreamed of seeking a bathroom, but you could never find it. The dread if you ever thought of running water or water flowing from a tap. The anguish when watching a movie and forgetting to go to the bathroom beforehand because you drank too much soft drink. I was trying so hard to keep it together.

Why did we have one bathroom?

“Sorry, Valeria,” I heard Nathaniel reply in a sing-song voice. “But you can’t rush perfection.”

“Perfection, Perfection! You’re fucking immortal! You don’t age!” I raged, and laughter erupted behind me.

“You might as well go to a public,” Neil snorted. Spread out on the leather couch, with his phone in hand and smiling like an idiot.

I gave the vampire an infuriated look before focusing on my shoes, wearing my warm orange dragon slippers. They clashed against my fuzzy purple dragon onesie. I looked out to the balcony and saw Brooklyn outside, unbothered by the elements. He tried to water his plants, but the violent wind carried the liquid away, unable to reach the roots and the leaves swayed in one direction, unable to withstand the gust's vicious power. My eyes landed on the temperature gauge, the single digits cruelly laughing at me.

"I'd rather take my chances waiting," I mumbled, starting my dance once more.

"What's so important that you need me to rush?" I heard Nathaniel's muffled voice behind the door.

"I need to pee!" I screamed back, still hopping from one foot to the other.

"Really, Valeria, must you use such vulgar expressions? Couldn't you be more ladylike?" I heard Nathaniel whine.

I banged my head on the door.

"This isn't the seventeenth century anymore!" I yelled and felt the sliver of hope dissipate into despair.

Neil laughed even louder. "Thank god, I'm not human anymore."

I hate my life.

'If you want an answer, yes, I finally got to the bathroom.'

The internet had been my greatest nemesis. The hours wasted with the endless opens tabs of gameplays and theories, my assignments start pile upon each other one by one.

"Valeria?" I recognised the British voice behind me, but I didn't react. Too focused on the latest video game theory about animatronics and why the killer murdered all those children. Footsteps echoed in my small, dark room. My heart rate increased as adrenaline crept into my veins. The light outside made me screech and shield my eyes from the natural light, hissing at the evil, cancer-making ball known as the sun.

"How childish," tutted the voice. I blinked the pain away, and the blurred figure before me came into view.

Nathaniel stood over, his cream jacket and white pants contrasted by the black shirt. I snort out a smile; he reminded me of a quirky Dalmatian. "Is this what you have been doing?" he asked, pointing to my laptop. "Watching ghastly things on... this - this thing."

"It's called a laptop," I corrected him.

"I don't care," he huffed and directed his attention to me. "I barely see you leave the house!"

"I'm on break," I defended.

"You crawl out of your room for food and only for food," Nathaniel continued, ignoring what I just said. "And." He stopped himself and sniffed. "You haven't showered in days!" he cried.

"So?" I asked.

"So, you need to get up and shower. I cannot have you in this state!" he exclaimed.

"Why? It's not like I'm going anywhere!" I hissed.

"Why? As a lady, you need to socialise, get out there, and find a suitor," he explained. I glared at the posh vampire.

Something in me snapped at that.

"Listen up!" I began standing on my two feet. "I have been busting my ass going to uni, working ridiculous long hours, for months! And just when the holidays come around, I have enough holiday to take time off!" I snarled, marching over to the door. "So, get your ass out of my room and let me live my life in peace," I hissed, holding the brass doorknob and directing Nathaniel out of my room.

Nathaniel stood there like I had slapped him. It took the vampire a moment to collect his thoughts, opening his mouth to speak, but closing it again. An icy gaze fell on me, anticipating I would retreat in fear. However, I had been living with him for so long that I knew his threats were idle, and he shied away from getting physically involved.

Hence why Nathaniel and Brooklyn worked well together.

Realizing I wouldn't retreat, he sighed and dragged his feet against the hardwood floors of my room.

"At least consider a shower," he huffed and skulked out, and I slammed the door behind him.

I sighed. The crumpled papers, dirty laundry, and scattered tech accessories made navigating my room feel like an obstacle course.

Maybe I should clean it.

Raising my arm, I could already smell the stench of two-day body odour. I gagged and threw my arm back down.

I need a shower.

Blog 9–Part 1

Date: June 1st
Time: 12 AM

'I had some questions relating to the boy's past. Living with them, I have learnt bits and pieces, but not a great deal. A vampire's past life as a human is apparently sacred? I guess. All I know is, when they tell you, it's a great honour and I have been curious myself but haven't had the guts to ask.'

The broken brown boxes stared me down. I could hear them laughing at me from the highest shelf in my tiny little closet. My patience grew thin every time each time I stretched my hand towards them, only to fall short. My office chair provided little help, and I was the only one home every time I made an attempt. But today was when it all changed. Brooklyn was home, and I could use his tallness to my advantage and slay the boxes in my closet once and for all.

Feeling the pride and exhilaration rise in my chest, music by gods played in my head. I felt like a warrior about to embark on a great battle against good and evil. Staring down at my enemy, sword in hand, armour glistening from the dancing flames, and once more, I faced my foe in one last battle of the greats. An urge to capture that moment pushed me to my laptop.

"Brooklyn!" I yelled before racing back to my work.

"What!" I heard his shout off in the distance. He was on the balcony.

"Can you help me for a second, please?" I cried out. My fingers were like rapid fire on the keyboard, typing the grand battle in my head. Cries of war and bloodshed played out through the written word.

I heard feet tapping behind me and felt the sharp bristles of Brooklyn's beard tickle my neck.

"You want me to help with writing?" he asked me, and I shook my head, still typing.

"No, there are these boxes in my closet that need taking down, and I'm not tall enough," I explained.

Brooklyn's ticklish beard was gone from my skin, and I heard the tall vampire sigh. Typing my last piece and returning my gaze back to the vampire, I watched him wrestle the boxes out of their place. With one last heave, he yanked them out. The fragile cardboard ripped apart, and all of its contents came out like a beast throwing up.

I need to add that.

Resisting the urge to type more, I helped Brooklyn pick up the scattered items. A book caught my interest, its blue plastic cover glistening in the sunlight.

Photos, ancient photos. One dating back a hundred years. Some were Nathaniel in the sixties and dressed to impress, as always. A few of Brooklyn showed him in the grunge look, and some of Neil in the nineties, one of him giving the bird.

I found one of all three of them backstage at a concert. Nathaniel overdressed in glam rock attire. Both Neil and Brooklyn dressed in leather jackets and plain shirts. I snorted, shaking my head. Nathaniel was overcompensating.

The back of the photo read, 'Kings Concert, 1985.'

"How did you guys get backstage?" I asked Brooklyn, showing him the photo.

"God, I can't believe we wore that," He snorted and shook his head after. "But to answer your question, Neil did. He just invited us along." Brooklyn handed the photo back and inched closer to me, looking over my shoulder.

I flipped through the photos. Brooklyn began to point and explain moments behind the picture and how they ended up there. But he stopped, and his smile disappeared. I followed his gaze and saw a black and white family photo. Brooklyn was standing tall and proud, in uniform, surrounded by his family members. A banner hung in the background. 'Goodbye, Brooklyn.'

“That was my last day at home,” he murmured, his thumb rubbing against the face. “To be sent over to Europe and fight in the war,” he continued. “My family never got to know the truth. I never said goodbye to them.”

“What happened?” I whispered.

Brooklyn cleared his throat and looked back at me with a sad smile.

“It’s a long story, but I can give you the short version,” he huffed out a laugh and wiped a stray tear from his eye.

-----(\(•vv•)/)-----

Blast those Nazi bastards!

I had curled further into the trench as another explosion went off. Dirt and debris spilled over into the ditch.

Too close! Damn it.

The trenches echoed with the clipped of gunfire, blood-curdling screams, and mournful cries. The canal was a grotesque tapestry of fallen soldiers' remains, the air heavy with the mix of decay, burnt gunpowder, and lingering smoke from explosions. Not even the sun's rays could pierce through it.

I squinted, trying to make things more transparent, but, of course, to no avail. Why did I think this would work?

I took a deep breath, loaded my gun, climbed up the ladder, and fired into the enemy line. The heavy fog created dark shadows, ones to give you nightmares for days. A few of my comrades left the safety of the trench and charged forward. They shot a few down before making it to the other side, and others jumped back in for safety, screaming at the top of their lungs. I held my position, trying to give them as much cover as possible.

A grenade landed on the ground near me. I jumped off the ladder and heard the ear-shattering boom. I landed on the hard, muddy floor below. The wind knocked from my lungs, struggling to get air back into them. The world rang sharp in my ears, stars bubbling in my vision. I moved onto my back, coughing as I inhaled too much smog. A familiar face rushed to me. Their mouth moved, but all I heard was the sharp ring in my ears.

Jacob?

He tried to lift me off the ground, grasping my khaki shirt with shaken hands. His stare went straight through me, and his mouth still moving. He pointed deeper into the trenches. The ringing was subdued, explosions erupting, and Jacob's voice was a muffled mess.

He got me to my feet, and his words shot through clear as day.

"Fucking Run!"

A dark silhouette emerged from the fog at a slow, steady pace. A Nazi soldier stared us down with hungry red eyes, his gaze piercing our souls. His mouth was covered in blood and large fangs hanging from his upper jaw. The creature crouched, his fingers turned into sharp claws, and snarled at my comrade and me. I didn't blink; the thing was gone like a mirage in the desert.

Quick as a bullet leaving the barrel of a gun, Jacob was gone from my side. The smog surrounded me, creeping in. I searched the dark crevices, the muddied floor, and thickened air.

"Jacob!" I screamed. Gunfire, explosions, and the screams of men only answered my plea. "Jacob!"

My feet moved, my heart in rhythm with each step. I screamed Jacob's name, looking around the muddy trenches, turning tight corners, and dodging bloody bodies.

My feet snared on an unknown body beneath me, and I fell to the muddy ground. Drenched in mud, I forced myself up, cursing the earth. I recognised the curly blonde hair and dark brown eyes. Jacob's throat torn out, and blood coated his face. Every emotion that flooded through me caught in my throat.

"J-Jacob," I whispered, crawling over and lifting his body close to mine. "N-no, C'mon, you-you can't be." A sob wracked through my body. "You gotta be alive. You have to. Everyone's waiting for you, your ma, your sisters, the girl you plan to marry!" Tears streamed down my face, cutting through the mud and grime. "They need you!" I cried. "I need you!" Sobbing into his muddy shirt, clenching my teeth, and swallowing the pain down into my gullet.

Curse them, curse them all to hell!

"Tried as he might, but the boy died as he failed." The noise quieted, allowing me to hear the thick German accent behind me.

Wiping the tears from my eyes and grabbing the knife hidden in my boot, I rose to my feet. My breathing evened, and my heart beat with courage. I gripped the handle even tighter and swung towards the monster behind me.

He grasped my arm. All the strength I could muster in slicing his throat was useless. The creature laughed at me and grabbed my wrist, plunging the knife into my throat. A sharp gasp escaped my lips, and blood filled my mouth. I gasped for air and spluttered onto the creature's face. He licked the specks off, eyes blazing with a deep hunger, gnawing away his sanity. With his long canines bared, he grabbed hold of the locks of my hair and yanked it back before sinking his teeth into my shoulder. The searing pain burned as teeth tore into muscle, and the agony of the knife was a whisper. I heard the creature gulp my blood. Illicit moans escaped from its throat, and it pulled me closer.

I pulled the knife from my throat and dug it into the creature's throat. Blood sprayed out from his jugular, splattering all over my face and entering my mouth, discovering the sweet heaven landing on my tongue. It sickened me at first, but ignited a beast deep within me.

It felt like an old friend, someone who I hadn't seen in years. A piece of me locked away, waiting to be let out, patiently letting me find my way back to it. It welcomed me with open arms, and I welcomed it in return.

The creature dropped me, ripping the knife from his throat, and plunged the bloodied knife into my chest. Everything dimmed around me, my eyes became heavy as if someone tied weights to them, the boom of war played, and time slowed around me. My body relaxed as the sweet release of death crept in.

Blog 10–part 2

Date: June 2nd
Time: 12:30 AM

"Then, what happened?" I asked Brooklyn. The vampire took a deep breath and closed the photo album. He put it back in the box and got up from the hardwood floor. He gave me his hand and a weak smile.

"C'mon, let's get some fresh air. I've been inside for too long," he announced. I nodded and took his icy hand, and he pulled me up from the hardwood floor. Brooklyn moved ahead of me, releasing a calming breath as he reached over the threshold. His hands continued to shake.

The crops on the balcony looked bigger than the last time I saw them. He had obviously taken great care of the plants.

Brooklyn sat down and stared at the city view.

“A lot happened after I woke up,” he continued.

🩸🩸-----(\(•w•)/)-----🩸🩸

Pain pulsed through my body as if someone had set me on fire, and all I could do was lay in the flames. My mouth felt full, sharp stabbing on my bottom lip, and a horrid ache in my upper jaw. With each hollow breath, it felt like needles were piercing my lungs. My hands twitched. My motor functions were uncontrollable. I couldn’t eve’ force my eyes open.

For hours, the pain persisted as I drifted in and out of consciousness.

Muffled voices, all of them incoherent, pulled me closer to my waking mind. The loud thrumming, the beautiful melodic beat, and the rich, heady aroma enraptured my senses, aching deep within my lungs like poison and promising me sweet relief if I drank from the source. The burning intensified, the hypnotising melody pounding louder in my skull. Clarity overtook.

Like a switch someone had flicked on, my body was ready to function. I struggled to breathe, feeling the burning in my lungs with each gasp. My visions blur as my breath quickens. Trepidation clawed its way through me, and my stomach rising to my throat.

"You don't need to breathe," an elderly voice called out. I counted three large concrete walls surrounding me and a barred wall before.

A cage? Am I in a cage? A cell? What is going on?

I steadied my breathing. The same inviting aroma overcame my senses, grounding me, comforting me. The sweet scent lit a dull ember, and before I knew it, it burst into an inferno, crawling underneath my skin once more.

My mouth was dry, and my lips felt cracked like concrete. I swallowed as if I had been drinking sand. My trembling hands inched closer to my mouth, feeling the sharp points. A biting sting ran through my finger, and I stared at the ruby bead welling on the tip. I fixated on the ruby jewel as the bitter iron overwhelmed my senses, and I brought the bloody tip to my lips. Just as it smelled, it was a tad bitter, but tasteless. It did nothing to dull the flames.

A deep longing grew in the pit of my stomach and clawed into my chest. I could feel it, that urge, that desire, that need. A demand soaked into my bones, begging me to act and satisfy from within.

"Are you with us?" the same voice asked. My eyes landed on the elderly gentleman outside of the cage. Very little light entered the room, and it astounded me at the clarity. I saw the brown thread of his jacket, the faint stains of red on his grey slacks, scuff marks on his black boots. No longer did they shine in the sun's light. Tired grey eyes stared down at me, his face clean-shaven, thick silver hair mopped on top of his head, and the thudding pulse under his wrinkled skin.

Something is not right.

His mouth moved, but all I could hear was the loud, rhythmic thumping once more. The yearning ate away at me. Sweet, warm, promising, every nerve inside burned, all with a single demand for the hunger to be sated. The gentleman took a step back with a knowing smile, just out of my reach.

Like a man stepping on a twig, I snapped. Letting out an inhuman scream, my fangs bared, ready to strike upon the soft flesh. With each intake of breath, my mind spun and twisted, fixated on quenching the desire burning in me. Each passing second felt like my mind was slipping into insanity. I grew frustrated, forcing myself through the bars, squeezing my torso through as much as possible.

My prey smiled at me, mocking me. Fury washed over me, leaving me screeching between bars and snapping my teeth at him.

"I need it! Damn it, come closer, let me feed!" I screamed internally.

The prey clicked their fingers, alerting more prey to come into the room. I felt woozy. My head pounded to the beautiful rhythm, the intoxicating aroma became too much. I felt my fingers ache and sharpen into dangerous claws, ready to slice the soft flesh and feast.

Six rounds of hot metal tore and burned into my flesh. I collapsed to the floor, clenching my jaw, holding back the scream in my chest.

Blood pooled from the wounds, leaking through my khaki shirt, staining it a deep red. The horrible, tasteless, bitter blood coated my tongue, and the primal urge in my chest grew. Every muscle tensed as a growl rumbled deep within my throat, and everything came reeling back. The beast hid away inside, and I didn't want it to. I wanted it again, this nature, this instinct. A piece of me was hiding. I yearned for it to come back.

Fuck!

I stared up at the man in front of me, the smile never leaving his lips. Head back-and-forth of the cell trying to piece what has happened.

I was there and now, here. How? Did I even move?

I grasped the cold metal for stability, letting the pain course through my body.

"What happened to me?" I whimpered.

"Back with us, I see?" I raised my head, meeting the man's eyes. A cruel twinkle lived in them, followed by a sadistic smile.

"What happened to me?" I repeated, my voice resolute.

"It's simple, son. You're a vampire," he replied. I laughed like a madman.

"A Vampire. No, this is all a joke. It has to be," I kept laughing.

"This is no joke, son. A vampire attacked your unit, but worse, a Nazi vampire," he pressed further, and I stopped. Vivid memories of that day flashed in my head. Everything I knew was mute. There is so much more to this damn world, and I am a part of it.

"What's going to happen to me?" I asked him as I stared at the ground, unable to look at the man before me.

"Unfortunately, we cannot let you out, ins-."

"What!" I slammed against the bar, and his armed men were ready to fire once more. "You can't keep me in here," I hissed.

"Oh, but we can," he assured.

"I fought in this damned war for my country, and this is how you treat me!" I screamed, my voice bouncing off the concrete walls, repeating my last words.

"You're not human anymore," he replied. "Brooklyn Hawkson died in battle on August the eighth, nineteen forty-three." A cold sensation crept from the nape of my neck, down to the small of my back, making me shudder involuntarily as I stared dumbfounded at the man.

"Y-you can't," I whispered. "I'm still me."

"Oh, are you now?" the elderly man signalled one of his soldiers to come closer.

I watched in morbid curiosity as the soldier exposed the skin on his arm and sliced into the flesh. My legs shook, and I crumbled to my knees. The erotic smell bled into my body, focusing on the delicious red liquid seeping from the wound. Yearning to taste and lap up every drop. I swallowed the non-existent spit. My body moved on its own, desperate to drink, to satisfy this cruel need burning deep within me. I growled as the soldier stepped away.

No.

A frenzy in my mind began, like a shark in the water. I thrashed against the metal, slamming into it, squeezing myself through the bars, forcing them to bend and break, all while I was snarling, screaming. The man clicked his fingers again. More bullets tore into my flesh. I fell onto my knees once more, feeling the part of me curl up and hide. Yearned to have it back, to satisfy it. I felt so incomplete.

"You died, son. You're not a soldier, you're not human, not even a US citizen." It felt like someone tied a rock to my heart and let sink into the abyss as I listen to his words. "Get comfortable. You will be here for a long time," he finished and stepped away with his two bodyguards, both aiming their guns at me while walking away.

The metal door shut and locked. Leaving me alone with my thoughts.

🩸🩸-----(╲(•ᵥᵥ•)╱)-----🩸🩸

Brooklyn's gaze fixed intently on his palm, his lips pressed together in a tight line, lost in a world of his own. His Adam's apple bobbed and took a sharp breath in. His hands shook as he swam deeper into his thoughts. The world around him no longer existed.

I grasped his icy hands, grounding Brooklyn back into reality. He looked into my eyes, and I could see fear, desperation, hopelessness mixing to create a horrible concoction of negativity.

"Whatever they did to you, it wasn't right. None of it was," I whispered to him. Brooklyn swallowed again and nodded.

"What they did next," he whispered. "It still haunts me to this day."

Blog 11–Part 3

Date: June 2nd
Time: 1AM

"They tortured me for months," Brooklyn whispered. His eyes became distant, with a lingering haunted expression. "They wanted to know how they could kill a vampire, how to weaken it. What made us tick? And they subjected me to every kind of experiment." Brooklyn took a deep breath in. "I struggle to remember the finer details, but two things stood out amongst my memories. The pain and hunger."

♦♦-----(╲(•ᵥᵥ•)╱)-----♦♦

Laying buck naked before scientists, I felt like a small rat surrounded by a group of vultures. A growl rose in my chest, and I bared my teeth at the leader. I watched as he retrieved one of the surgical knives with his gloved hand.

How long had it been? How long had I been trapped down in the horrid dark cell? Alone with my thoughts of the kill. This rabid hunger was digging away at my sanity, slipping like an oiled eel through my fingertips.

Blood, so much blood.

The lead scientist, wielding the surgical knife, was a tall man, always dressed in white scrubs, surgical mask, thick brimmed glasses adorning his slender face.

"Experiment three, subject is still temperamental," the southern accent rung in my head, and the surgeon shone a blinding light. I squirmed in my restraints, snapping my teeth and snarling a warning. Stay away. "Still sensitive towards the light." He sighed, his gloved hand forcing my left eye open. “Eyes have returned to a normal pupil. The colour of the iris is grey.” He spoke carefully, and his assistant scribbled down every word.

“Cross-referencing to the journals, today we shall test snake venom. Potent to humans, dangerous to vampires. Hunters of old had described the vampire to be overcome with agony when injected into them. A way to weaken the vampire,” the surgeon prattled on.

I felt the surgeon’s cold needle enter, injecting what felt like molten lava into my veins, spreading like liquid fire and spreading through my muscles.

I thrashed about, pulling against the restraints. The chains rattled and banged against the steel table. The surgeons all backed away, watching with careful eyes. Gasping for air, I screamed as the pain became unbearable.

♦♦-----(＼(•ᵥᵥ•)／)-----♦♦

Brooklyn clenched his jaw together, squeezing my hand like a vice. I gritted my jaw, watching my fingers turning red, trying to ignore the pain. Brooklyn looked back at me and down at my hand. He released his grip and let go.

"Sorry"" Brooklyn muttered. I breathed in and flexed my hand.

"It's ok. You can stop if you want to," I assured him, and Brooklyn shook his head.

"It's ok. It's best if I talk about it," he murmured, nodding to himself.

♦♦-----(＼(•ᵥᵥ•)／)-----♦♦

His fingers closed around my heart and I lurched forward, snapping my teeth at the man. "Grasping the heart causes the subject to flinch," the head surgeon announced, and his assistant scribbled down her notepad. “Let’s see if they can survive having their heart punctured.” He grabbed a wooden stake and stabbed it into my heart. Blood sluggishly spurted out from the wound, pain shooting deep into my core, and I jerked forward in a silent scream. My voice gave out an hour before as they sliced and diced through my lower abdomen. I shook, agony consuming me, as I lay with the stake protruding from my chest, wishing my life would fade away from a piece of wood. Some smiled at my pain as they observed me. “Well, it seems Mr. Stroker is wrong,” the surgeon cracked, and his legion of followers laughed. He ripped the wooden stake out, and I breathed in relief. Feeling the organ stitch itself up, but skins flesh forced open with metal clamps. The surgeon placed his bloody gloves all over my face. Although it was my blood, the dizzying smell consumed all my thoughts.

"Nurse, how long did it take for the liver to replace itself?" The surgeon's eyes flicked to the nearby nurse, brows raised in query.

"About two days, doctor, and that was without blood," the nurse informed him. The surgeon nodded, grasping the surgical knife, bringing the sharp edge closer to my eye. I forced myself into the table, wishing I could mould and become one with the metal. "Let's see how long it will take for his eye to grow back."

🩸🩸-----(\(•̀ᵥᵥ•́)/)-----🩸🩸

I swallowed and breathed. Rage shook through my body, pleading for a way to time travel and beat those surgeons senseless. Brooklyn didn't deserve the torture. He didn't deserve the pain. What cruel fate decided he must go through this? What universe believes people like him to suffer? Brooklyn put his hand back on mine.

“Those fucktards,” I whispered.

“You can say that again.”

‘How long has it been?’

I couldn’t remember. Life in that cell, the days blurred together, and time became mute. I was ravenous by that point. So weak with hunger and desperate for the taste of fresh human blood, I became a shell of my former self. I could not keep my body upright, left slumped against the concrete. Not having the energy to move, let alone control my thoughts, I couldn’t keep my dreams of the hunt at bay.

There was no peace, only pain.

Blood. Needed blood. Blood, please someone. Blood. Let me taste it. Just taste it. Pain, so much pain. Just taste. Please. Blood, need blood!

"It won't stop." I looked over to the figure stepping from the shadows. A perfect mirrored image of myself smiled down at me. "They won't give us what we want," it explained, walking closer to my broken form.

Who?

"I'm you, well, the part of you that wants to tear into human flesh, gorge on every drop of blood, inflict pain, and suffer on those who have done the same in kind," the other Brooklyn explained. "A manifestation of your frustration, the beast that wants to be unleashed, the awakened piece of your soul wanting out," it told me with great pizzazz.

'Why are you here?'

"It's simple. You've lost your mind."

"I don't get it." I frowned, my brows knitting together.

"Get what?" Brooklyn asked me.

"You mentioned you felt this missing piece inside you, explaining it was your nature, whenever you couldn't indulge it. Did you feel complete when you became a vampire?" I asked. Brooklyn sat back and thought about it for a moment, scratching his beard and humming.

"I'll start by saying knowing about our existence, you have only just scratched the surface of the supernatural. There is an entire process that determines the balance of the universe, and who becomes a vampire is tied into that."

"What process is that?" I asked him. Brooklyn sighed and looked over at the potted trees in the garden.

"There are certain pre-determined factors that contribute to humans seeking out vampires. These factors may include a person who doesn't enjoy socialising with other humans, has had a tough upbringing within their family, or has faced rejection from their own kind. Unaware, they instinctively gravitate towards us. While they may feel uneasy on the surface, deep down, they are aware of their kinship and comfort in the presence of vampires," he listed and then tapped his nose. "If someone teaches you. You can just smell them out. A faint hormone lingers in their blood, telling us you're one of us." He smiled and looked back at me. "Those are factors we look for, but not all of us know this and risk turning the human into a feral," Brooklyn sighed.

"A feral?" I asked.

"A human who shouldn't be a vampire. They lose their soul and become a mindless beast."

"Wait, wait, wait," I shook my hands. "You're telling me that vampires have souls?" I cut him off. Brooklyn gave a fanged smile.

"We sure do. We were born with these souls. That is how we are different," Brooklyn answered. I held my head in my hands, feeling a little overwhelmed by the information provided. "I know it's a lot to take in," Brooklyn soothed, and placed his hand on my shoulder.

"I know... I'm just surprised, and curious, like why? Why so much effort to have only certain people with souls like that? Why make it hard for vampires to find them and turn them? Why does such a process exist?" I raised my hands up as the weight of my questions pour out. Brooklyn smiled and ruffled my hair like I was eight.

"I don't have all the answers myself, but I'm sure someone does." I nodded and took a deep breath.

"Do you want to know how I escaped?" he asked me, and I nodded my head.

"How?"

"I didn't."

Blog 12–Part 4

Date: June 2nd
Time: 1:05AM

During his time in France, Nathaniel would weave through whispered conversations, his eyes always alert, his ears catching every secret, in hopes of ascending the social ranks among the European covens. He wasn't sure yet which one to choose.

"This poor man," Nathaniel wept, re-reading the reports over and over. "Thrown away like a used washcloth and hung out to dry." Nathaniel couldn't even bear to look at his finished meal without heaving back up the precious life he had solen. A young sergeant boy, a puppet for the higher-ups, but a delicious plaything.

Nathaniel grabbed the maps and layouts of the facility. The war was still raging on. Security would be tight, but nothing a bit of stealth couldn't fix. He scanned the document with his own eyes, praying for his memory not to fail him on this rescue mission.

-----(\(•vv•)/)-----

"Wait, Nathaniel saved you?" I cut Brooklyn midway. He chuckles and scratches the back of his neck.

"Sort of," he replies, his lips turning into a wry smile. Brooklyn's shoulders shook, his laughter barely contained as he struggled to keep a straight face. "From what Nathaniel told me, leading up to the rescue–he got captured himself," Brooklyn giggles. "He left his capture out and waited to be rescued by another coven from France. They filled me in the rest of the story." Brooklyn is in hysterics by this point.

When I think about it, it sounds like something Nathaniel would do. Attempt a solo rescue mission, seen as a hero amongst the covens. Who would attempt this, you ask? A vampire who is so reckless as charging into a military facility to claim fame and social status would.

Oh, Nathaniel.

Brooklyn's laughter soon became infectious, leaving a smile on my own lips. It's a pleasant change from his sullen look, which I hated. I never want him to see him like that again. He calms himself down, smiling at the memory. At least some good has come out of this nightmare.

-----(ヽ(•vv•)ノ)-----

Stirring from my sleep, feeling the soft, cotton material underneath my fingers, the warm weight hugging my body. This isn't right.

Snapping my eyes open and rising from the soft, bouncy floor underneath me. I assessed the surrounding area. No longer was I trapped by three concrete walls and iron bars, hidden in darkness and brought out for experiments. I sat in a smaller room, dark green walls, a horrific creamy rug, and a brown pine door cantered on one wall.

The familiar scent of iron-rich blood wafted through the air. My fangs ached, and my body burned with hunger. I drew my eyes to a glass of blood sitting on the bedside table. With care, I reached for the glass but halted when I heard a snort across the room.

A gentleman slept in a wooden armchair in the farthest corner of the room. I took in the man's sun-kissed skin, and neatly trimmed goatee that framed his chin. *Is this another experiment?* I thought. I looked back at the glass of blood again, hesitant to even drink.

Memories flashed, all resurfacing to the forefront. I remembered the reflections of the time where I was tied to the metal table. Surgeons and nurses, slicing, injecting, ripping into my skin. Pain aching deep within my nerves, setting me alight. Panic crept in. The walls seemed to move closer, closing me in. There was nowhere to run.

I couldn't escape. I was trapped. This was a test, an experiment, a simulation. None of this could be real.

I curled into myself, unable to stop shaking, letting the tears run down my cheeks, while my mind repeated this single sentence.

This is a lie. All of this is a lie.

"Hey," a voice soothed and touched my arm. The familiar, comforting red, the slit pupil of a fellow predator. We were the same. "Good to see you're awake.

Thought you would be out another month." Words failed me. His voice carried a British accent, catching me off guard.

The Brit nodded to me and looked at the glass of blood. He picked up the glass and took a whiff of its contents. He scrunched his nose and put the glass down. "All coagulated. I told them it wouldn't be nice when you woke," he huffed and looked back to me with a grin.

"Is this real?" I asked, my voice hoarse from all the screaming and lack of use. A deep chuckle rumbled from the vampire, his moustache bouncing with his lip.

"Of course! I'm real, just as you are," he chuckled. "What made you think different?"

I remained silent. Trembling once more, memories flashed in my head again. Scattered all over the place, fragments and pieces jutting out, making me question reality. What is real and what is fiction? Is another a dream of the hunt, only for my prey to slip from my fingers again or a twisted experiment? Which memory begins and which one ends?

The Brit's smile disappeared. He put his hand on my shoulder once more.

"It's ok. You don't have to say anything." He assured. More tears broke free, salty and wet, and they streaked down my face.

"I'm free?" The two words I thought I would never speak. Freedom, I am free.

"You are. I got you out. You're free," the tanned vampire assured, resting his hands on my shoulders.

"Thank you." The vampire smiled and removed his hands. The tanned vampire sniffled, refraining from crying himself.

"Now, you hungry?" he asked. I could only nod my head in response. "Good, you made a mess a week ago in the facility, and then passed out. I suspected you would be when you woke." The tanned vampire explained. He shook his head and moved to the pine door. "I'll go tell them you're awake."

Once more, I was alone again with my thoughts and felt a little more at ease before looking back at the glass of blood.

I grasped the glass and inhaled the rich ambrosia. The aroma consumed my senses, my mouth salivating, and fangs growing in my jaw. I noted the thick layer on top of the liquid, ignoring it and opened my mouth. I welcomed the cold contents. Moaning as its rich flavour hit my taste buds, revitalizing the cells within, sating this cruel desire, but only for a bit. I licked the insides, desperate for the remaining contents.

Pulling the glass away from my lips, I savoured the lingering taste in my mouth. Only one thought remained.

I. Am. Free.

Blog 13

Date: June 5th
Time: 9pm

'Heyo! So regarding the last four chapters, thank you all for your kind words for Brooklyn. He has been through a lot. I feel for him. I just had to give him the biggest hug once he finished his tale.

I shall learn the rest of my roommate's stories, but life must go on for now.'

Writing, writing. I needed to do more writing when I got home.

I tapped my foot on the vinyl floor of the restaurant entrance, ignoring the loud chatter, the clinking of glasses, the clashing of cutlery, the chefs yelling, and the waiters stressing over served food and tableware—I was, unfortunately, one of those waiters. The difference between them and me was passion. While others chatted about the thrill of their last shift, I dream about leaving this hellhole. Each day I work in hospitality, I reminded how much I loathe human society. The number of entitled individuals I have served who believed the world owed them something is painfully high. I also thought living with three vampires may have added extra loathing for humans, but we wouldn't go into that now.

My job was to seat people at their tables. That was my role, my job, my sole existence, and I hated it. Sure, I had no passion for this job. That was why I was not getting many hours, but I was also the oldest out of all the wait staff. The youngest was eighteen.

I inhaled and exhaled, looking through the long list, searching through the names on the reserved table. It was pretty tedious, words skewed from left to right. There was no order, all but chaos and impatience.

"Right this way," I said, directing my customers through the restaurant. Crystal chandeliers cast a warm glow on the spotless crimson carpet. Cream curtains diffused the afternoon sun into a golden hue. Each table felt smooth to the touch, and dark oak chairs with plush red velvet cushions promised comfort.

The subtle scent of garlic and fresh herbs wafted through the air, and the Yarra River was visible through the expansive windows. The occasional clink of cutlery punctuated the room's soft atmosphere.

I admit I chose this place on aesthetic appearance. I hastily applied without reading the online employment reviews—a mistake I now regretted.

I seated the impatient couple, handing them menus and explaining the specials.

Just when I believed I had reached the safety of my box at the front entrance, I heard my name called out.

I spun on my heel, my eyes scouring the crowd, looking at the individual faces crossing my view.

"Valeria!" I stiffened at the voice behind me. Dread leered in the back of my mind. I recognised the long straight blonde hair, caked skin makeup, sharp acrylic nails, red lips, brighter than blood itself, and intense blue eyes.

"Sally, oh my god, hi," I said, bringing my arms out, and she embraced me into a hug.

Oh god.

"It's so good to see you! I haven't seen you since we graduated! You just up and vanished!" I gave a fake smile and nodded.

There's a reason no one knows.

"I can't believe it myself."

Where's Neil when I need him?

"So, what have you been up to?" she asked me. I stared at her, dumbfounded. Could she not see the uniform? Was she blind to the black shirt, pants, and a white apron?

"Working and uni. What about you?" I asked with a sickening sweetness in my voice.

"Oh, nothing exciting, just received a promotion and celebrating it over with my fiancé," she shrugged and gasped. "You need to meet him. He is just the sweetest!" she exclaimed, grabbing my arm and dragging me over to their table. My manager scowled at me as he passed both of us.

I was going to get reprimanded for this later.

A tall, muscular man stood and glowered at me, a quick flash of yellow in his eyes. He puffed his chest out and let out a small growl. I shrunk under his gaze, confused by the death stare.

What did I do?

"Cedric, this is Valeria!" Sally pushed me forward to her fiancé. He sized me up, his nostrils flaring and muscles tensing. I swallowed. My heart stammered as he continued to stare at me. "We went to high school together!" Sally exclaimed, unaware of her man's sudden hostility.

I put my hand out.

"I-it's nice to meet you," I stuttered.

Cedric's chest rose and fell with a slow, deep breath, his face betraying a storm of emotions before he nodded, as if convincing himself of something. He put his arms out and wrapped me in a hug.

"Oh, he's a hugger." I gave Sally a weak smile.

Someone, anyone, please end me.

'I said one day I would tell my story. Why I was desperate to live with a bunch of vampires? Why, no one knew where I went. I left the state to get away from everyone, but of course, no one can run away from their past. For now, all I can say is one dead parent and the other addicted to alcohol.'

I heard yelling on the other side of the door when I arrived from work. Brooklyn had been throwing things across the apartment, while Nathaniel had tried to calm the plant-loving, flannel-wearing vampire. I stood at the door, deciding if I wanted to step in or find a place for the night. Was I in the mood to put up with them all?

Before I could decide, the door cracked open, a bright beam of light entering the dark hall, illuminating the space. Neil's head poked through, providing much-needed relief for my eyes. I adjusted to see his trademark sullen look, and he greeted me.

"I wouldn't come home tonight if I were you. I expect those two to be going at it all night. But enter at your own risk. I just suggest you stay in your room," Neil forewarned me. I weighed my options.

Option one, I spend my hard-earned cash in an expensive hotel or stay awake in my room all night and go to uni exhausted.

Ok, Valeria, you can do this.

I put my hand on the door, giving it a slight push. Neil took this as an answer and moved out of the way. The door creaked open, and the muffled screaming intensified, like someone turned the surround sound on and put the volume on twenty.

Neil closed the door and stood close to me. Brooklyn, in a blur of motion, darted after Nathaniel, who narrowly dodged every grab. The curly stache vampire was trying everything in his power to calm his bearded friend, but it all fell on deaf ears.

"What are they fighting about?" I asked Neil on the side.

"Don't know. Walked into this five minutes before you did," Neil replied, and we watched Brooklyn launch himself across the couches and just miss Nathaniel.

"I can't believe you dragged us into this!" Brooklyn screamed, getting up from the hardwood floors.

"Uh oh, Brooklyn rage," I murmured, giggling to myself afterward.

I needed to go to bed.

"What?" Neil snapped.

"Oh, it's an internet joke. You won't get it," I replied and shrugged it off.

Neil frowned at my answer and exhaled out of frustration. I watched the vampire next to me sniff the air like a cat, his nose upright, trying to understand the scent he was inhaling. His head snapped to me, his eyes glowing in a fiery rage. Neils prowled closer, and I stepped back, pinning myself to the oak door, wishing I could phase through it. Neil's face was near my neck by this point. Inhaling deep, he snarled and flinched back. Fangs exposed, his hands turning to claws, eyes blinded by pure hatred, and his body rigid and tense.

"Where the fuck is it?" he snapped.

"W-what?" my voice cracked. Shaking like a leaf, my heart ramming against my chest, all signs screamed to run.

Both Nathaniel and Brooklyn stopped their fight, looking toward us both and sniffing the air. Brooklyn's face turned to stone, and his body tensed. Nathaniel moved to Neil and put his hand on Neil's shoulder with careful ease.

"She doesn't know, remember?" Nathaniel reminded Neil. Neil kept his gaze on me.

"You reek of dog," Neil hissed. "Go for a shower and get that stench off you," he ordered, turning away, disappearing into his room, and slamming the door. Silence fell on us all.

What just happened?

'I thought vampires were going to be the only supernatural I faced when living with them. That wasn't the case.'

Werewolves. They exist, they hate vampires, and kill anyone associated with a vampire.

Guess who was on the hit list? Me! Hello!

There were two types of werewolves, just as there were for vampires. Vampires were more complicated, whereas werewolves were far more straightforward.

Feral werewolves had no control over their form, and they consistently killed. Purebred werewolves were the primary reason feral werewolves existed. The purebreds used the ferals to fight against vampires. For the unfortunate victims who survived an attack from other feral werewolves, purebreds were born. Either parent or both had to be purebred to produce an offspring. Purebreds could control their form, use their intellect when shifted, plan, and chase their prey.

Neil sat on the armchair farthest from all of us. His eyes stared at me. I could only guess he was picturing the werewolf's death or mine.

"There is a werewolf problem here in Melbourne," Nathaniel sighed. "Hence, why I accepted the "

"Yes, but you left out nominating me to fight for your battles," Brooklyn hissed. "I told you, I am done fighting!" he snarled.

"I just thought you would agree." Nathaniel shrugged.

"Without consulting me first!" Brooklyn raged.

"They only respect vampires who can fight!" Nathaniel whined, but his explanations fell on deaf ears.

"I don't care! Leave your social goals out of my life!" Brooklyn continued to scream.

"We're going," Neil interjected. "All of us."

"Since when did you care?" Brooklyn growled.

"I don't give a fuck about Nathaniel's social goal. If there are fucking werewolves in my city, I want to be the one slaughtering them," Neil glowered, and Brooklyn backed down.

They all calmed down, and a peaceful silence filled the apartment once more. Outside, skyscrapers channelled a wind that howled with the lonely cries of the city.

"Bright side, it might be fun for you guys," I shrugged.

"You're invited too," Nathaniel replied, his voice dulling to a whisper.

"I have to go, don't I?"

Blog 14

Date: June 6th
Time: 10AM

'Heyoo! Gosh, so many questions about me and my life. I wasn't expecting such interest. I never really thought my past is worth mentioning, but when I am ready, I will talk about it. My past may catch up to me sooner if I show anything.

Anywhore, please enjoy the ramblings of my life.'

There was a saying that went around among Melbourne residents, believing it only stayed amongst them as they lived with this day by day. But any traveller who visited and lived outside of Melbourne knew this saying very well.

Melbourne, a city to have four seasons in one day.

I swear when I last looked up from my phone, it was sunny. Not a single cloud was in sight. It was enjoyable to feel the sun's rays while leaning against the glass on the balcony door.

A sudden gust of wind whooshed through the balcony, carrying dark clouds that blotted out the sun. The first drops of rain splattered against the glass as I pulled the door shut, plopping onto the cold leather couch. My teeth chattering. Wrestling with the fluffy blanket I left out for this purpose, I wrapped it around my body.

Be one with the blanket, be warm as the blanket.

My eyelids felt like they were weighed down with bricks, each breath shallower than the last. I struggled to keep my eyes open. I pulled my hand free from the confines of fluff, ensuring no warmth could escape from the makeshift hole, and stared at my phone.

I heard the balcony door slide open and Brooklyn's familiar humming. His wet feet tapped against the hardwood floor. The smell of fresh rain hitting the earth gave the delightful aroma of petrichor. He continued humming, opening the fridge door, and pulling out a blood packet.

Brooklyn tore into it, sipping the contents as he walked out of the kitchen, passing the lounge and heading back to the balcony outside. I heard the rain pelt down even harder against the roof.

Nathaniel's gonna have a conniption fit when he comes downstairs.

My phone dinged, redirecting my attention to the message. I snorted and replied.

"What's that goofy smile for?" Neil asked, dropping onto the couch next to me. I kept my phone close to me as Neil tried to look over my shoulder.

"None of your business," I replied, ignoring his attempts. Neil huffed and leaned over me, just like an annoying big brother.

"Must you do this?" I asked him.

"How else shall I make your life a misery?" he responded with a sneer.

"I hate you," I grumbled.

With a spring in his step, Nathaniel stepped down the steel spiral staircase and headed to the kitchen.

"What the!" Nathaniel cried out. He stepped out and followed the trail out to the balcony. He stood at the door, staring at the torrential rain pelting outside. "Brooklyn!" Nathaniel yelled, and the apartment filled with Neil's laughter. "Don't let him back in, he is all wet," Nathaniel huffed and stomped back upstairs.

"Don't let the puppy in, got it," Neil giggled.

Before Nathaniel left, he stopped and pointed to me.

"Don't you have a date tonight?" Nathaniel asked. My heart skipped a beat. I felt Neil's gaze harden on me as I opened my mouth.

"Yeah, we're gonna meet up for a movie. Nothing too serious," I shrugged it off.

"Ah, wonderful. Well, it's good to see you trying," Nathaniel praised and proceeded upstairs.

Old school ideologies.

“A date, huh?” Neil grunted, moving away from me and sitting on the other end of the couch. I looked away from my phone and saw him staring at the coffee table. His face hardened like stone, and his eyes were glassy.

“Yeah, I just thought–I -.” I stumbled over my words, looking back at my hands. I got nothing.

“Is he hot?” Neil asked.

“I–uh–well–I guess,” I answered, shrugging. “He’s got a pleasant face to look at, but hot–I care, but like it’s a bonus if they have a wonderful personality... god, why is this complicated?” I exhaled into my hands before rubbing my temples.

Someone end me.

Neil nodded and got up from the couch and went to his room. Each tick of the clock seemed to echo in the empty space in my chest, and the growing guilt seemed to build with each passing second. Why did I even feel this way? He wants to kill me all the time.

'I had a date. I wanted to surprise you all with this information but, it didn't turn out like I hoped it would.'

The cold had found a way, seeping deep within my bones, chilling my skin, turning me blue. Winter was cruel, cold, and unbearable. I missed the warm confines of my room, but there I was, standing on the sidewalk, outside the movie theatre. The night sky was clear, and I could not see a single star. The city life was bustling and alive. Cars flew by, the concrete path filled with people or some vampires, maybe some werewolves.

Panic crept up my spine. Memories of the night they explained werewolves to me, the day I met Cedric. I was at risk.

I tried to rid the thoughts swimming in my head. It was funny how I had gotten used to their threats and promises of death. I knew it would never happen by their hands, but the thought of someone else it terrified me. Living with those three numbskulls, I felt safe.

I looked at my phone; it was seven-thirty.

Any second.

My stomach churned as if a swarm of butterflies had taken flight, my foot tapping an anxious rhythm on the concrete. Each beat of my heart felt like a drum in my chest, my tongue sticking to the roof of my dry mouth.

Any moment.

Enormous crowds gathered inside, buying popcorn and drinks, tickets in hand. The wind was icy, and I felt it biting. I checked my phone's time, and he wasn't here. I swallowed and sent him a message, checking if everything was okay.

Couples left the theatre from an earlier showing, hand in hand, enjoying each other's company. I watched, wanting the same thing. A person to share my life with, someone I could rely on. It was cheesy, but I always wondered if soul mates existed, or something like "the one." It would be nice if I had that, but of course, in the land of the twenty-first century, this hopeless romantic would wait for quite some time.

Speaking of time.

It was past eight already. I received no reply to my message. My heart sank.

'five more minutes.'

'I was hesitant to write this, but–something interesting happened afterwards.'

The door creaked open. Sniffling the moisture from my nose, I turned and looked at the perpetrator.

Neil walked in. I watched him brace the door to reduce the noise and winced as it closed with a click. He stopped in his tracks, realising my existence as our eyes met. Remembering my tear-streaked face, I looked away, rubbing my cheeks to get rid of the wet marks. I felt the cold fabric touch my skin as Neil sat next to me on the coffee table. Nathaniel would have a conniption fit if he saw us.

"Hey," he whispered.

"Hey," I replied hoarsely.

"How did the date go?" he asked, sounding earnest. I shrugged and swallowed.

"He didn't show," I murmured.

My gaze fell on the garish white rug beneath the coffee table and before I knew it, the dam broke once more, and I unleashed the warm, salty tears cascading down my cheeks. "I don't get it," I whispered. "Am I trying too hard? Am I too eager? Do I jump the gun? What am I doing wrong?" I asked whoever was listening, whether it be the universe or Neil, to answer back.

“Some guys are just assholes,” he answered. “Few do it to avoid the truth of not liking you, others do it for laughs.”

“It’s always the first one,” I croaked. “Boys don’t like girls with short hair. They like girls who dress prettily, act like damsels, and look feminine. That’s what the boys are interested in.” I sniffled. “Boys think you’re a lesbian with that haircut. You’re ‘one of the boys.’ Why would anyone ever find you attractive?” I mimicked the voices of others’ opinions. With each encounter and rejection I got, I only believed these words even more. “Who would anyone ever love someone like me?” I murmured.

“You’re not ‘one of the boys’,” Neil whispered. “There are moments you are ‘one of the guys,’ but there are also moments where I see you gushing over a poem or a sweet moment between people. You love the flowers Brooklyn grows and the dresses Nathaniel bought you, and don't lie - Nathaniel told me you went to a store that had a particular look you liked." It was true. I did. Modern Victorian clothing is something I liked.

"I also see you yearning for romance. You don't give guys a day if they are after sex. You seek genuine connection. That makes you, you. I like that about you."

I wiped the tears away and a small smile crept over my lips. The pain in my chest eased into a slight sting. It was still there, but bearable.

"Thank you."

'It was the first decent moment I had with the young vampire. I don't know if there will ever be another, but I can only hope.'

Blog 15

Date: June 10th
Time: 4:25PM

'Thank you all for your kind words. Connecting with you all, sharing your stories and your happy endings. It gives a girl like me hope.'

Ever since Brooklyn had achieved his minor success in gathering us all around to watch a movie a few months back, his next goal in the 'getting Neil to hang out' endeavour was a planned get-together, one involving the botanical gardens, on one of the coldest days of the year.

Now, I'm sure you're wondering how he convinced Neil? The answer: me. I was made the bait, unaware of what they had spoken about, but in the end,

Neil had agreed. I could only imagine I was being used as a bargaining chip to be eaten by Neil himself.

"See, isn't this much better?" Brooklyn asked us, map in hand, leading the group through the grassy field and ignoring all the concrete paths, taking us to the rose garden. I shivered as the cold brisk wind sliced through my winter clothes, freezing my organs.

"It would be if I weren't freezing my ass off," I chattered. I crossed my arms into my body, trying to keep all the warmth in as I battled the cold. Nathaniel walked closer to me, using his extra puffy jacket to keep me warm. We looked like walking penguins by this point.

"Oh yes, wonderful," Neil added in, dragging far behind.

Apart from me, Neil was the only one who dressed appropriately for winter. Brooklyn and Nathaniel were yet to understand the concept of 'cold.' Brooklyn led along with a spring in his step. Wearing brown sandals, a white singlet, and black board shorts that reached down to his knees, he sported sunglasses on his forehead and a broad smile graced his lips.

"Can't you smell the fresh air, the beautiful flowers, or hear the bees buzz by and the people laughing?" Everyone stared at Brooklyn like he was a madman, odd looks from passersby, whispering if the bearded man was even cold.

"Their hearts are beating, their blood gushing, painting all the roses red. Screams of agony as I tear them all limb from limb," Neil lips curled into a sadistic grin as Brooklyn's face fell, another precious moment sabotaged. I gave an exasperated sigh. Nathaniel mulled over Neil's words. I could tell he was picturing himself feasting on the flowing blood.

Speaking of Nathaniel. For someone who was dressed in suits and fine waistcoats, this was the moment he failed. Shocker, I know.

Nathaniel looked as if he was ready for Antarctica. No, a ski resort, and it was minus fifteen degrees. A big puffy marshmallow jacket, woollen beanie covering his ears, ski gloves, thick blue pants, and snow boots to add. Regardless of overkill, he seemed saner than Brooklyn at this point. Neil and I were in trench coats, long pants, and gloves, feeling like the only ones who had checked the weather forecast that morning. We looked normal and were a part of the twenty-first century. But I had to admit, I was willing to trade my coat with Nathaniel's.

Brooklyn stopped and turned, stalking back to Neil.

"Must you ruin such a nice day?" Brooklyn hissed, grabbing Neil's coat.

Neil bared his canines in retaliation, which, of course, made Brooklyn expose his back. Nathaniel and I looked at each other and rolled our eyes.

"All right, break it up, you two," Nathaniel stepped in and pushed them away from each other. "Let's try to have an enjoyable time, all right?" he huffed and walked back to the garden entrance. Brooklyn and Neil gave each other one more death glare and resumed their normal appearance.

The Melbourne Botanical Garden was a sanctuary within the city, a lush tapestry of colourful blooms and towering palms. Birds chirped melodiously, complementing the rustling leaves. Gravel pathways led through diverse flora, from formal European designs to untamed Australian bushland. Iron-wrought lampposts and wooden benches added a Victorian charm, while hidden streams and the perfume of myriad flowers enriched the sensory experience. The gardens offered a peaceful contrast to urban life, an oasis of natural beauty and calm.

Neil walked beside me, and Nathaniel walked beside Brooklyn, pushing them apart as much as possible.

"Valeria!" All four of us froze as we heard my name called out to the heavens. A chill ran down my spine once more.

Oh god.

I turned to the perpetrator of the voice. Sally, her arm waving in the air as she ran towards me, was ecstatic to get my attention.

Four million people in this goddamn city, and I run into her again! Why couldn't it be Senpai instead?

Before I even took a step forward, Neil pulled me closer to his chest. Sally slowed in front of us. An amalgam of shock, inquisitiveness, and elation washed over her. She attempted to piece together two puzzles that did not fit.

"Oh, my god!" she gushed, taking a step closer. Neil reacted by bringing me closer and growling like a wild animal. Sally was, of course, unaware as always. "You didn't tell me you had a partner!" she squealed.

"W-well ac-."

"Neil," the vampire cut me off and introduced himself.

"Sally." she shook his gloved hand with enthusiasm.

"What brings you here?" I asked through my clenched jaw. Feeling desperate, I tried to speed the situation up as much as possible.

"Oh, you know, finding the perfect venue for the wedding," she giggled, and her eyes widened.

Please, no.

"You two should come!" Sally squawked. "Why didn't I think of that sooner!" she exclaimed to herself, like she had just solved the world's most complicated math problem. "I'll send you a message on chat and let you know when the dates are." She continued, not giving a chance for any of us to speak.

"Sally!" we all heard her name being called across the gardens. Neil growled in his chest and he clung to me tighter.

I can't breathe at this point.

"Oh, that's Cedric. Better get back to planning. It's great to meet you," she said and wrapped us both in a hug and ran off to her fiancé. Neil watched as she disappeared into the gardens. His icy gaze never left the path, and he continued to cling to me. He growled into the air as a warning.

"I smell like a dog now," he hissed.

"We should head back," Nathaniel interjected, snapping Neil from his predatory gaze. Neil looked back at me. His eyes softened, and he let go. Taking a deep breath of air, I felt a sense of relief as I could breathe freely once more.

"Sorry," Neil murmured. None of us said a word on our way back home. Brooklyn, Nathaniel, and Neil were all tense and alert, ready for an enemy attack. All eyes were scouring the crowds. Neil remained at the back, Brooklyn at my side, and Nathaniel led the way. Odd whispers from the crowd caught my attention, wondering if I was someone important. I shrunk under their gazes and kept my eyes down.

I guess it's time.

I had said little since we arrived home. We each retreated to our own corners, our faces betraying a mix of tension and fear we weren't willing to voice.

Sitting outside on the balcony floor, I looked over the shining city of Melbourne, listening to the sounds of car horns and sirens in the distance. The frosty air swirled in the night, sapping all the heat the sun had left behind. Shuddering, I curled up into a ball, thinking back to the warm sunny state I hailed from. I missed Queensland. I missed Brisbane. Things were warmer up there and less... no, it was crazy here, just as it was up there.

I heard the glass door slide open and close behind me. Brooklyn was asleep in his hammock, leaving me with two guesses.

"You haven't said a word since today. Are you all right?" the familiar British voice asked. Of course, Nathaniel would ask. Why I expected Neil to be the one to do so? Raising my head from my little ball, I placed my chin on my knees, contemplating the situation. I continued to stare back at the luminescent city.

"Remember the day we first met?" I asked him. Before sitting himself next to me, Nathaniel wiped any dirt from the tiles.

"Of course," Nathaniel smiled softly. Looking down at his hand, he reflected on the events of the day, contemplating their significance. A foolish human wandering in their little abode.

"Would you have really killed me if I had no one?" Nathaniel knitted his brow together, lips pursing and lost in his thoughts. He remained silent for a few minutes. "You could have killed me on the day we met," I added, breaking him from his own trance.

"If we wanted to get caught, yes," Nathaniel answered carefully, but I shook my head.

"No, I mean, if you had done that day. No one would have known," I corrected and watched

Nathaniel's mouth fall open. "I left home as soon as I graduated, worked and travelled my way down south. No one knew where I went. I'm alone and no one would have ever known it was you guys. Even with the ad, no one knew where I was, and I wanted to keep it that way," I explained to Nathaniel, ignoring his question altogether.

"Seeing Sally just brought up a bunch of terrible memories, and I just put you guys in danger. That werewolf knows about me, and now the three of you," I murmured. Nathaniel cleared his throat, staring back at the cityscape.

"Why are you telling me this?" Nathaniel asked, and I shrugged my shoulders.

"Don't know. Trust maybe, holding onto this foolish sliver of hope that you guys care. I felt if I told the truth, maybe there's a chance." I took a deep breath. Feeling the tears well up. "It's odd. I feel like I found a place where I belong, but since you know the truth, my life is now in your hands." I gave a dry chuckle and swallowed the tears away. "So I have three endings to this situation, and I do not choose how they end." I raise three fingers. "Ending one, I leave this apartment when you want me to, of course, and never see my face again." One finger goes down. "Ending two, you kill me, hide my body and no one would know." Another finger. "Ending Three, the good ending. I stay here. But again, it's up to you three."

Nathaniel remained silent, taking a calming breath, and the noise of the city below replaced the silence as Nathaniel gathered his thoughts.

"After the party," he spoke. "Then we'll decide your fate." I nodded at his last word.

Blog 16

Date: June 15th
Time: 8:17AM

It was midnight when I came home from a crazy shift at work. They called it full moonitis, and werewolves weren't the only beasts to roam at this hour. Weirdos and strange occurrences appeared when the full moon was present.

Leaning back in the elevator, I stared at the steel floor, feeling tempted to sit down and rest my aching feet. Each floor I passed felt like an eternity, my feet throbbing with every ding. The trip was five minutes, but I was dramatic when I was tired.

I stepped out into the hall, hearing murmurs behind the large oak door. I took a shaky breath, my ears straining to catch a familiar tone among the murmurs, begging some entity. They were not fighting right now.

Three pairs of eyes landed on me, all gaping at me like I was some tentacle beast.

What did I do?

Brooklyn growled, crouching towards Neil. I took a step back, and the situation sank in. Nathaniel had told them the truth. Neil grinned, dodging Brooklyn's leap and charging towards me. I headed for the elevator, desperate to escape, but my human reflexes were useless against a vampire. The youngest pinned me to the floor of the hallway. His fangs were on full display, long and sharp, close to my neck.

"Told you I would drain you dry," he whispered in my ear.

A sharp, burning pain dug into my neck. I clenched my jaw shut and swallowed down my cries of agony, and refused to give this bastard any satisfaction. I focused on my breathing, shutting the pain out of my mind. Neil's fangs sink even deeper, tearing through muscle and tendons. He growled, gasped, and moaned as he drank my blood in heavy hot gulps.

"Let." I snapped my eyes open and saw Brooklyn looming over Neil, hot fiery rage burning in his eyes. "Her." He grabbed Neil by the back of the neck, and a loud sickening snap of Neil's spine echoed my ears. "Go!" Brooklyn shouted. Neil let go, gasping in pain, coughing up my blood. Brooklyn threw him back into the apartment, crashing into the hardwood floor with a loud thud. Brooklyn hoisted me up from the ground, carrying me inside and freaking out over the wound on my neck. “Nathaniel-Nathaniel, get a fucking bandage!” he snarled, putting me on the couch.

Nathaniel ran around like a mad chicken with its head cut off. He dashed from cabinet to drawer, flinging items aside in a frantic search for something, anything, to staunch the bleeding. Vampires didn’t need medical treatment, something they never had to consider until living with a human.

'I'm ok, just surprised.'

“They act like nothing happened.” Nathaniel breathed a sigh of relief. I touched Nathaniel’s makeshift bandage, comprising tea towels and tape. I nodded, swallowing a small amount of water from the glass Brooklyn handed me.

"Like it never happened," I croaked, wincing at the sharp sting.

"Are you alright?" Brooklyn asked me, placing his hand on my shoulder. I nodded, putting the glass down next to me and getting up from the armchair.

"Yeah, just going to head to bed," I replied in a whisper, passing the two 'mother' vampires down the dark hall to my small, dank bedroom. I closed the door, locking it, and slid down onto the cold hardwood.

"Why did you tell him?" I heard Brooklyn hiss at Nathaniel with a burning intensity that could scorch the sun.

"I didn't expect him to act like this," Nathaniel defended himself. "I wanted to tell you all in confidence."

"With shit like this, you tell me and me alone!" Brooklyn screamed.

"I-I-." Nathaniel stuttered.

"Neil will snuff out anything that will make him open up, and you gave him the opportunity with your big mouth," Brooklyn yelled even louder.

"What?" Nathaniel snapped. I heard Brooklyn snarl at Nathaniel.

"I have been trying to get him to open up for years, trying to help him see we can be his family, his coven, but he has stubbornly resisted for years!" Brooklyn explained. "We know nothing about him. We find him ripped to shreds, on the brink of death, we bring him into our lives, and for what? He treats us like shit. He doesn't listen, doesn't respect our wishes, brings live food to our home, putting us at risk. And we try to be welcoming, try to be understanding, but he keeps us out, not letting us slither in." I heard Brooklyn groan.

"If you hate it that much, why don't you kick him out?" Nathaniel asked.

"There were times I did, but he refused to leave. I know he cares, but he refuses to show it. I want him to open up!" he yelled. "And then," Brooklyn's voice turned into a whisper. "Valeria turns up and years of work I have tried to put in, she puts the cracks in his armour in only three months." The corners of my mouth twitch, warmth spreading across my face despite the tension. "He's changed so much since she's been here, and he knows this. That's why Valeria terrifies him."

"You are more observant than I am, my friend," Nathaniel began. "I still don't understand how Valeria can affect him that way?"

"She's not normal. Just think about it. Some human, desperate to find solace, crazy enough to fall for this ad, desperate enough to be living with creatures that prey on her kind and still find comfort in our presence. Aren't those the signs or things or whatever this fucked up universe makes it out to be!" Brooklyn raised his voice.

"And the scent. Only a handful of vampires can identify it, and it's something that requires training," Nathaniel added his two cents' worth of evidence. "What do we do now?" Nathaniel asked his old friend.

"All we can do is wait." He replied and then silence. I thought the conversation was over until I heard Nathaniel whisper one more thing.

"It will work out."

Blog 17

Date: June 18th
Time: 6:30PM

'Thank you all for your concern. I'm alive and well I shouldn't be surprised that this would be his reaction, but yet somehow, I am. Thank you for private messages to leave and get out, and you are right but... something deep down is telling me not to leave.'

I leaned back in my chair, and my words failed, lost in a scrambled mess within my head. The human part of me was screaming to run and get out of there while I had the chance, but there was this other half. Telling me to stay. That's if I left. I would not have the same opportunity as I did then. But what opportunity was there? Having a home and living with three crazy vampires? What did any of this mean?

I left home to get away from the mess my life had somehow ended up in. I wanted to get away from the nightmare. I opened the top drawer, grasping the wooden photo frame.

“Things were better when you were here, dad."

'My father was a paramedic. He took great pride in his job, cared about saving lives and died trying to save someone else. Their drunk friend attacked him with one coward’s punch, killing him on the spot.

It's an immense problem to this day. Still, drunken idiots attacking emergency officers while they are trying to save a life. It's infuriating!'

My eyes stung. A knot formed in my throat, but I refused to let the tears spill. Maybe they were right. Their discussion last night might have had something to do with this. Maybe this messed up universe had a reason for me to be here. Was it indeed fate?

The walls seemed to vibrate from Brooklyn, and Neil's screaming match. With the amount of noise these boys created, I'm surprised they hadn't received a warning or a police call yet. Brooklyn alternated between a command to apologise and a biting insult aimed at Neil's intelligence. Shouting phrases like 'what the hell are you thinking?' or 'are you that fucked in the head?'

Points to Brooklyn for picking up on our lingo.

"Until this party, you will not be alone with her," I heard Brooklyn's muffled voice from the other side of my door. Two vampire hens yelling at their unruly teenage son.

"One of us will be here with her at all times," I heard Nathaniel add, backing Brooklyn up.

"You gotta be kidding me. She's just a human!" Neil snarled. "Why the heck are you protecting her?" The thud of Neil's footsteps moved away, culminating in the harsh slam of a door. Silence fell, thick and final. I could guess they didn't have an answer of their own.

I closed the drawer and rose from the comfort of my bed. Making my way towards the oak door, I strained to hear the two mother hens.

"You can come out, Valeria," Nathaniel called out. I peered from the edge of the door, using the wood to shield myself. Keeping the distance between the vampires and me, I felt like a five-year-old getting caught by her parents for eavesdropping on their argument.

"Looks like we have a lot to discuss." Nathaniel's eyes met mine, heavy with a promise of uncomfortable conversations to come.

Blog 18

Date: June 19th
Time: 12 AM

'I said I would tell you all my past and I think its time. Why did I leave QLD?

Though I gave a brief story about my dad, I never mentioned about my mum.

My relationship with her was a complicated one. As much as I loved her, she wasn't the same after he passed.

I remember the drunken days after I come home from school, three bottles of vodka gone and a packet of pain killers mixed down. I would find her passed out in the bathroom or unconscious on her bed. She would be so heavily medicated should would sometimes wet herself.

Month after month, I would pour out the bottles, destroy the pills, argue with her, plead with her, beg her to get help, but she wouldn't.

Mum got so bad her family ignored the problem, pretended she was fine and push her away. They didn't need the mess in their lives, but as a result, they discarded me as well. Alone, dealing with a mother who relied on me and not the other way around.

I cooked us dinner, cleaned the house, drove mum to appointments, trying to get her the help she needed.

Dad's super and life insurance kept us afloat for all my final years in high school, but as I drew closer to graduating. Things didn't get better.

I remember coming home, putting my bag down.

I remember the eerie silence of the house.

I remember creeping to her bedroom door.

I remember the sickness in my stomach, and the dread lurching up my throat.

I remember opening it, the fan still running and her body...so stiff.

I remember how cold she felt, how her chest didn't move.

I remember it all. Stained in my head and I cannot get rid of it.

Graduation was a blur. I didn't want to attend and watch my peers be with their happy families. So with that, I got my certificate and left. Slowly over time I made my way down south, never looking back.

I miss them both and while I am still angry at my mother, I still loved her. I just wish things were better between us before she passed.'

Blog 19–part 1

Date: June 25th
Time: 3:17PM

'Healing from this is a journey. Some think it would take a few months, a year, but grief is not like that. It's a wound that heals but turns into a scar. It bleeds and bleeds till it aches and then slowly, over time, it dulls. While I was angry at my mother, I never stopped loving her.

Thank you for reading my previous blog. I hope it gave some insight. Enjoy the new update.'

Okay, I'll admit, I look forward to our dress shopping sessions, where Nathaniel and I would pour over silk and satin as though they were ancient scrolls. It was our peculiar way of bonding, and although we bickered about my choices, I gained insight into the haughty vampire's character. Though his face remained stern, his eyes softened whenever he saw the smile on my face or how my eyes light up at my interests. He took the time to ask questions and listen to every enthusiastic word.

We wandered until Nathaniel's eyes lit up at the same time as mine—both of us spotting something we liked in the window. A style I very much preferred, and the choices were limitless. Nathaniel approved, of course. I ran my fingers through the selection of beautiful gowns to try on, but winced when I flipped the price tags.

One attempt after another, Nathaniel snubbed his nose upwords at every suggestion made by the shop assistant. His keen eyes scrutinising at the choice of fabrics and colours, tutting at the quality of the dresses.

In the end, the assistant gave up and left us alone, much to Nathaniels' pleasure. I caught a group of young teens exchanging amused glances, then chuckling behind their hands, clearly entertained by our argument over colour schemes. Even the soft classical music trickling from the overhead speakers seemed to amplify, rather than mask, our heated discussion. My eyes darted past the racks of clothes and landed on walls so shockingly pink they clash against the checkerboard vinyl floor. It almost hurts to look at.

"I don't see why I have to shop for new clothes," I muttered, looking at my reflection in the mirror. I scrunched my nose in disgust at the idea of wearing this purple frilly thing, also known as a dress.

"I want you to wear something more colourful than your black funeral clothes," Nathaniel explained as he handed me another dress. At least this one was a lovely blue, but again, it had too many frills.

"Why not? I'm going to a party full of vampires. I might as well save everyone the effort and wear black for my casket," I said. Nathaniel rolled his eyes and passed me some heels.

"I'll be there, and so will Brooklyn. No one is going to kill you."

"You sound very confident," I retorted and slinked back into the changing room while Nathaniel stayed outside. There was a brief pause before I heard him clear his throat.

"Because we–well–I have grown fond of you," he admitted through clenched teeth. It sounded as though he was wrestling with the words. I popped my head from the curtain with a cheeky smile.

"Sorry, what was that? I didn't quite catch that. Human hearing and all." Nathaniel smiles, catching on.

"I said you're the worst. I look forward to them eating you. Never again," Nathaniel mocked. I laughed at his over-the-top pompous accent and went back to trying on the dress.

Still isn't my thing.

I came out a few seconds later, looking into the mirror, still unsure about the look and style. Nathaniel's reflection showed him approaching from behind and he hummed.

"I'll go find another one," he insisted and went to the rack.

"How are you so good at this?" I asked him while taking the high heels off.

"Having three older sisters can do that," Nathaniel shrugged, still looking.

"I didn't know you had -."

"You didn't because I didn't tell you," Nathaniel cut me off.

Right, so much for being polite.

"They would always ask for my opinion, dragging me to the markets insisting I help pick an outfit for the next ball," Nathaniel prattled on. "Much to my father's dismay, of course," he mentioned while he continued looking for a dress. I moved away from the mirror and looked around the dressing rooms, ensuring no ears were listening in. I came back to Nathaniel, who was mulling over a red dress in his hand. My mouth dropped, a strapless red dress with black lace decorating the red silk flowing down to the floor.

“Try this on,” Nathaniel handed me the dress in a sing-song voice, knowing full well I had fallen in love with it.

“Thank you,” I whispered, and rushed back into the small room, pulling the thick curtain dividing us. “So, how did you become a vampire?” I asked, struggling to take the blue dress off. I heard Nathaniel chuckle.

“Would it be cliché if I said it was a man and a careless night?” he answered with a question. I popped my head out from the curtain again, seeing Nathaniel’s smug smile.

"Nathaniel living with you for months, nothing phases me," I replied and stuck my head back in, wrestling the dress off.

♦♦-----(＼(•ᵥᵥ•)／)-----♦♦

Nathaniel knew he wasn't like other men. While others were busy making a fuss over how ample their bosom was or how small their buttocks were. Nathaniel found the appeal more in the company of men. Caught between the sacred hymns that shaped his faith and the irrepressible longing for another man, Nathaniel felt both a euphoric ache and a searing guilt.

His mother had forced him to go to church every Sunday morning, listening to the horrid priest prattle on. Nathaniel shuddered at the memory, feeling both thankful for his newfound ability to make decisions as a man and despising the responsibilities that accompanied it.

The only son, the sole inheritor of the estate and business. With his other sisters married off to chosen suitors, Nathaniel would be the only one to choose a partner or, in his father's words, 'a bride.'

Marriage? I am not ready for that. Nathaniel thought, shaking his head. He knew he was lying to himself, but to believe the lie, he must become the lie. And here he was, at the old church. He was surprised to see it still standing, considering how ancient it was. The old bricks had cracks, the wood appeared to be rotting; the weather abused stone, the distinct smell of wet mould lingered in the air, and its tiles uplifted and sunken from the shifting ground below.

Nathaniel sighed, shifting in his seat, moving one butt cheek to the other, feeling his back ache against the hardwood and cursing the inventor of the church pews. The Priest looked as if he was there of the church's construction, cough in his direction, and he would drop dead. His back hunched over, with wrinkles folding over his skin, his eyes murky as if they had sucked the life out of them, and more hair in his ears than on top of his head. He shook like a leaf, holding the bible close to his chest. A wry smile appeared as the newlyweds kissed and filled the church with celebration. Nathaniel refrained from showing his disgust, noticing the Priest's missing teeth.

Oh, thank God it's over. Nathaniel thought. Still surprised the church hadn't collapsed upon them. *If fate was kinder.* Nathaniel thought as he rose from his seat.

"Please remind me, who are these people?" Nathaniel whispered to his mother. She shushed him, waving the eulogy paper in Nathaniel's face, tutting her son to be quiet and then scanned the surrounding crowd. No one appeared to be listening.

"Distant relatives. And you should be grateful that they invited us," she explained.

"I don't even know these people," Nathaniel hissed. His mother shushed him once more and smiled at the surrounding crowd. His veins flashed with the familiar burn, frustration clawing at his throat, but for the sake of appearance, he kept his mouth shut.

-----(\(•w•)/)-----

Nathaniel glanced upwards, wishing for a bolt of lightning to come crashing down and strike Nathaniel. Standing beside his mother, wine in hand, drowning out the prattle between her, some other noble, and his young daughter next to him. *I need more wine.* He sulked to himself.

His mother always loved singing Nathaniel's praises, hinting her own son was available and single. It took everything in Nathaniel to hold his tongue and not snap and stomp away, and drinking himself into a stupor. Oh, how he would love to drink himself silly and forget this dreadful night, but of course, like any dutiful son, he promised. Promised to socialise and try to get to know the young ladies here, all in the name of making his mother happy.

Nathaniel could feel his skin crawl as the young girl before him. Her doe-like eyes were wide, besotted, as if he were some sort of Adonis. Which, of course, in Nathaniel's opinion, he was, but from the wrong crowd.

His eyes darted from one person to another, his brows furrowing slightly. A subtle grimace tugged at the corners of his mouth, revealing his mild distaste. Not because they were not pretty. No, it was what they were wearing. A fashion disaster, to be more precise. Some were out of date, faded, not as well-kept as most noble ladies in the city. In the cruel reality of the country, beautiful clothes were unnecessary. He cursed his sisters for giving him the knowledge of high fashion. His lip quirked up as he appraised every woman's clothing, forming solutions in his head, remembering the skills he had equipped himself with.

Then nothing. It was as if his brain had flatlined, the lump in his throat growing, unable to budge with each swallow. His heart skipped and bucked into a race. Gorgeous long curly hair, sparkling grey eyes, defined cheekbones, plump, kissable lips, a dazzling white smile, arched eyebrows, pale skin as if he had never seen the sun in his life.

Both their eyes met, and his hungry gaze froze Nathaniel in his place. The stranger gave a devilish smirk, eyes flickering to the darkroom and back, taunting Nathaniel to follow. The handsome stranger left the room, giving Nathaniel one more sideways glance.

His breath left his lungs, his heart now ramming out of his chest and mouth, his mouth becoming dry as a drought over the countryside. He hurriedly excused himself, plonked the half-filled glass of wine on the table, and ignored his mother's protests. Nathaniel followed the stranger out of the room, ignoring the odd stares given by the crowd. He stepped into a quiet room. More eyes looked at the man, but he ignored them, skimming the crowd, looking for the blonde god. Hope fluttered in his chest as he watched him ascend the stairs.

Nathaniel swallowed and followed soon after.

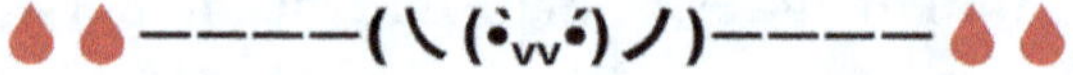

A pause soon came after. I popped my head through the curtain to check on Nathaniel. His eyes tinged with an unspoken sadness as his mind was buried in deep reflection. I wanted to step out and give the vampire a hug, but I was in my underwear, and I didn't feel comfortable stepping out.

"Are you ok?" I asked him. Nathaniel snapped out of his thoughts, clearing his throat.

"I-I'm fine," he lied. His hand shot up to rub his nose, and cleared his throat. "Now, are you dressed?"

Blog 20 Part–2

Date: June 25th
Time: 3:34PM

I glanced in the mirror, pulling at the fabric. My eyes narrowed at the slight bulge of my stomach, the burden of self-consciousness grips at my throat. My weight was decent. I wasn't overweight, but I wasn't skinny either.

I needed to eat better or exercise more, one of the two.

"Everything all right?" I heard Nathaniel's voice from the other side of the curtain.

"Uh, yeah," I mumbled, sliding the fabric curtain across the metal rod. Nathaniel's inquisitive eye draped over me and I involuntarily wrapped my arms around myself. He stepped back and assessed the dress, his arms crossed, one eyebrow raised.

“Something is missing,” he murmured to himself. Without a word, Nathaniel left for a moment and returned with another pair of heels, much shorter than the ones he handed to me.

“I hope I’m not overdressed for this party,” My voice wavered, each syllable tinged with the palpable tension. Millions of possibilities rush through my head. I become the laughingstock of the entire vampire community.

“You’ll be fine.” Nathaniel murmurs. “Back in my day, they would consider you underdressed."

🩸🩸-----(╲(•̀vv•́)╱)-----🩸🩸

Nathaniel would not let an opportunity like this pass by. It had been quite some time; it became an itch under his skin that had gone unscratched for far too long. If he could, he would peel his skin back, just to feel the relief.

When was it last, days? No, months. Nathaniel remembered the experience, but never the name or the face of those he shared a bed with. He approached, hesitant to make any sudden movements.

"Nathaniel, is it?" For the first time, Nathaniel was speechless. Did this man catch his attention on purpose? Did he just want a friendly chat? Was he lured here just to be robbed and murdered? Nathaniel narrowed his gaze, searching for some clue to the stranger's intentions. A fault in his smile, a side glance, a crease in his eyes, anything. The stranger chuckled, taking the silence as a yes.

"I have heard about you," he continued. Nathaniel blinked, his brain registering words and how to speak once more.

"And what could that be?" Nathaniel asked, wary of what they would say next.

"Oh, but a young man, three older sisters married, the heir to the family business and," the man paused, his icy hand touching Nathaniel's cheek, his lips drawing closer until they were touching. Nathaniel welcomed the cool kiss. His lips tingled as they pulled apart.

"Still single, yearning for freedom from the chains they have thrust upon you since birth," the Adonis whispered in Nathaniel's ear. A tingling wave cascaded down Nathaniel's back, making the fine hairs stand on end. It didn't take long for his neck to be adorned with kisses. Nathaniel eased, letting out an audible sigh. Relishing the cold sensations as his skin heated.

"I can free you from all of this," the man promised between kisses. Nathaniel gasped as he felt the suction on his throat.

"H-how?" Nathaniel's brain flatlined for the second time that night.

"I'll show you."

Nathaniel only remembered the pain burning into his neck, his skin torn apart, and blood leaving his body. Caught in the spiderweb, he felt the spider's teeth latch onto his neck. Nathaniel still kicked himself mentally over that night. To be caught in the hands of a predator, knowing his father would be more ashamed of that than having an interest in men.

Nathaniel remembered waking up in a cage big enough for two people. A young woman cowered in the corner, crying as she stared at Nathaniel in horror. Her pale face streaked with wet tears. His surroundings were unfamiliar to him. Not a single crack of light could sneak in yet. It was clear. Stone floor, wooden planks of wood nailed together to form these four walls. The musky smell of wet soil lingered in the air.

A cellar, how quaint. He thought bitter.

Every pulse sent a fresh wave of fire through Nathaniel's veins, each throb more agonising than the last. His own mind screaming for sustenance. Nathaniel sought the sweet smell wafting in the air. His thoughts swam in a murky haze, his limbs felt like lead weights, barely responding to his will.

Warmth, blood, need.

His eyes landed back on the woman, fixated on the beating pulse beneath her bosom. The mesmerizing sight entranced him, making him move on his own. A predator trapped with prey that could not escape. He could take as much time as he wanted, all to make the hunt much more satisfying. The woman scrambled further into the corner of the cage, screaming for someone to help her. Nathaniel's clawed hand grasped her throat, applying gentle pressure to her paper skin. He enjoyed the warmth radiating from her, the feeling comforting his cold fingertips. His nails made the tiniest cut along her throat and watched the red jewel well up before gliding down. Everything was dry in Nathaniel's mouth. Unable to look away from the crimson waterfall. His senses enriched him with the beautiful smell. It was driving him crazy.

He raked his sandpaper tongue across the delicate skin of her milky white neck, tasting the tantalising blend of fear and life. Tasting the crimson life, and the monster was free from its cage. Unable to contain himself, he struck the vein, like a viper, digging his fangs deep, desperate to drink every drop. A guttural moan rumbled from his throat, an electric shiver coursing through him as he drank. The warmth sliding down his throat and pooling into his body. But it was not enough. Nathaniel snarled, tearing his fangs along the flesh, creating deep gashes into the muscle. Snarling, he lapped up any drops left. He tried the other side of the neck, hoping for more to pool into his mouth, but there was nothing but a dry husk.

Nathaniel threw the body away in a fit. Growling at the dead flesh, he felt frustrated that it did not have enough. He wanted it to come back to life just so he could tear it limb from limb and make it suffer for not sating his hunger. The insatiable hunger gnawing at him, urging him to find more—now.

Heavy footsteps approached the cage, bringing Nathaniel out of his blood-induced frenzy.

"Well, I thought you would never wake up." Nathaniel tore away from the body, hissing at the creature. He remembered the blonde hair, the sharp cheekbones. His eyes no longer sparkled a beautiful grey but a terrifying crimson.

"I was worried that I drained you too much during your turning. I would have waited, but I prefer to keep my sanity." The creature smirked. Nathaniel growled at him, feeling his nails sharpen into deadly claws. He launched himself, swiping his hand through the bars, just nicking the skin of his cheek.

"Damn purebreds," the Adonis hissed. Nathaniel observed the skin healing, smelled something bad, and saw black blood dripping down. Nathaniel bared his teeth at the creature. He laughed at Nathaniel and regained his composure.

"No use wasting your energy. You're going to be in here for a long time," he taunted.

"What did you do to me?" Nathaniel hissed.

-----(\(•ᵥᵥ•)/)-----

Nathaniel remained quiet for some time. His lips parted several times, each aborted sentence etched into the taut lines of his face.

"Feral vampires are mindless creatures," Nathaniel spoke. "But there is a way for them to get their mind back. Their sanity, I suppose. They don't have the same loyalty as purebreds and will kill anything that stands in their way," he continued, swallowing. "Vampire blood is the answer, and drinking it keeps their minds. Very few figure this out. It's by pure luck, or another has fed them; therefore, we hunt them, or we become their prey." Nathaniel took another deep breath and looked into my eyes. His eyes held a tempest of anguish, waves of unspoken pain crashing behind his irises. "I was his personal blood bag for weeks."

Blog 21–part 3

Date: June 25th
Time: 4Pm

Nathaniel's eyes glazed over, lost in some distant world. He wore a contemplative expression, different from Brooklyn's visible pain but equally intense. The way he clenched and unclenched his fists made me think he was wrestling with inner demons. I fell forward off the chair and tackled Nathaniel into a hug. He stiffened, holding his footing. He wrapped his arms around me and sighed.

"Heh. I guess I needed this," Nathaniel mused to himself, holding on just a little longer.

"You told no one, have you?" I asked him, my voice muffled by his dress shirt.

"No, not even Brooklyn knows. I would hate for him to gallivant across the city and slaughter every feral he comes across," Nathaniel sighed and patted my back. I pulled away and gave him the best smile I could muster.

"How did you get out?"

Nathaniel shrugged, his eyes narrowing for a moment, as if trying to grasp a slippery eel before giving up.

"I remember what happened, and I know I am indebted to one particular vampire, though he does not care about debts. It is his... duty," Nathaniel explained.

-----(＼(•̀ᵥᵥ•́)ノ)-----

Nathaniel remembered the creature stalking him.

Its hungry gaze leered over Nathaniel like a predator sizing up its prey. The creature's eyes were a terrifying white, its canines overgrown, sharp and jagged like a shark. It had a nose that pointed upwards like a bat, and its clawed hands reached for Nathaniel. He backed himself into the farthest corner of the cage, desperately looking for a way out, a way to dodge this deformed creature.

Nathaniel evaded its swipe, attempting to make an escape for the entrance. But of course, his dreams of escaping and hope had to be crushed because his enemy was faster. He felt a weight jumping on his back, gravity pulling him down, crashing onto the cobblestone floor. He winced as he felt his skin tear upon contact. The feral on his back grabbed Nathaniel's brown locks and yanked his head back, exposing his throat. Dread pooled in the pit of Nathaniel's stomach, his dead heart shattering, dashing whatever hope he had left. He was so close, yet so far from escape. It hurt.

As he lay there, vulnerable, Nathaniel felt a chilling empathy for the humans he'd devoured, understanding their fear and helplessness. The burning pain erupted once more. Its teeth tore into his skin, ripping into Nathaniel's muscle. His stomach churned, listening to its sickening moans. His blood satisfied the creature, and Nathaniel tried with all his might, but couldn't throw the feral off his back. Each struggle tired his muscles, his vision blurring, and the creature pinned Nathaniel further into the stone ground. It felt as if a building had crushed him. With one last drink, the feral dragged its teeth along his throat, tearing it apart. Nathaniel wheezed, the unbearable burn and blood trickling from the wound. That's if there was any blood left in him.

The feral grabbed onto his mud-covered, torn dress shirt, dragging him back and throwing him. With a loud clang, the cage door slammed, and the feral snarled at little Nathaniel.

"Maybe next time you won't try to escape."

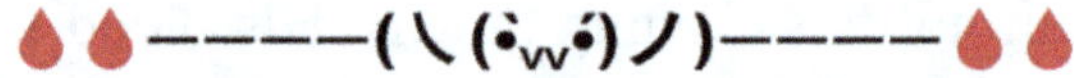

Rage vibrated through me, my body strung up like a violin string. I wanted to hunt the feral down myself, but I could see Nathaniel's reasoning. "Don't even think about it," Nathaniel warned. I gave the vampire a wide grin. "I do not know what you are talking about." Nathaniel hummed and rolled his eyes. "Sure, you do." It frustrated me that I could not time travel. You would believe modern science had figured it out by now, but of course, I had to sit here in the present and sulk. If time travel was possible, I'd first go after Brooklyn's captors, then Nathaniel's. I could picture it now, a mysterious stranger travelling to the past and righting all wrongs, a hero to the nation. I should write that down. "You're daydreaming again," Nathaniel snapped me out of my thoughts. I gave him a sheepish smile. "So, who is the vampire that saved you?" I asked, directing the conversation back to the story. Nathaniel blinked for a few seconds. It was obvious he had forgotten what we were discussing. "Right, the story."

💧💧-----(＼(•̀ᵥᵥ•́)／)-----💧💧

Leaning against the metal bars, the area on his back had gone numb against the unyielding surface. Nathaniel was thankful it no longer hurt.

It was the same vicious cycle every two days. Nathaniel fed, and the next day they drained him of his own blood. He had tried to resist, lasting only a few hours before succumbing to nature. The feral knew how to entice his prey. He couldn't help but breathe it in, to stare at the red waterfall. His thoughts filled with the taste, the heady ambrosia that followed when he drank, the satisfaction of the kill. It was a drug, a drug he needed.

Weakly, Nathaniel lifted his hands, tracing over the wound on his neck, feeling it stitch itself back together. He hissed as he pressed too hard on the wound.

Nathaniel would have chosen death, if this was to be his fate for eternity. Swallowing the non-existent spit, Nathaniel begged for some entity to rid him of this cruel existence.

He heard what sounded like three pairs of feet clunking against the hardwood. His prayers seemed to be unanswered, and he was going through this all over again.

Nathaniel hoped he hadn't brought any friends, dreading to be bitten all over his body.

"Check downstairs. There may be more ferals," he heard a deep voice through the wood, sending shivers down Nathaniel's spine. A presence emanated from the floor above him, putting him at ease, and he knew he was safe.

'It is him.' the voices in his head whispered. His own instincts becoming a separate being. *'Respect him.'* they whispered.

What was this sensation?

"Ah Syrus," a voice called out as the door opened. "You're not going to like this!"

Syrus, that name rings a bell.

"Syrus and his brothers saved me. If it weren't for them, I would still be down there." Nathaniel took a deep breath and gave a reassuring smile. "He took me to a coven nearby. Their boss's name is Trick. Clever vampire, strategic, always knew what was happening. Never make a bet with him," Nathaniel rambled on and got back to the point. "I recovered, but I never got to thank him, and when I heard he's based here in Australia. I booked the next ticket over, dragging Brooklyn with me. I want to repay my debt. No, not debt. I want to be part of his family, helping in any way I can," he explained. It was rare to see him this serious, determined for a cause. It warmed my heart.

Family, huh.

"Now c'mon no more talking about the past. We have some shopping to do." I didn't say a word, knowing he no longer wished to talk about the past. I got off the black and white vinyl floor of the clothes shop and helped Nathaniel up while doing so.

Throughout the rest of our shopping, Nathaniel was distant. His eyes had a far-off look, as if he were navigating through a labyrinth of haunting memories. Even my attempts to distract him were futile. He barely acknowledged the guys I pointed out to him, the elegant suits, novel series that I believed he would be interested in. Nothing seemed to work. In the end, we sat in the middle of the food court. Voices echoed in the vast open space, the smell of food mixing, creating a unique fragrance but enticing enough to draw the hungry crowds in. Nathaniel stuck with drinking a latte and watched me slurp down udon.

I freaking love udon.

Nathaniel watched me slurp down my udon with a disgusted expression, his eyes devoid of the curiosity or longing one might expect from someone faced with a delicious meal.

'That afternoon, Nathaniel opened to Brooklyn, who was surprised to hear about his friend's past, one he thought he would never learn. I watch him grow furious as Nathaniel told his story and swear to hunt every feral he could find. Nathaniel was right. The posh vampire looked more at ease as he and Brooklyn both shared each other's stories. Seeing themselves as a little family.'

Blog 22

Date July 2nd
Time 10pm

'Thank you all for the kind words. Nathaniel is doing better. He's getting more and more excited about the party as each day passes.

As I have been writing this blog for the past few months, I feel like I have veered off what it's like to live with vampires a bit and want to lighten things up. Has there been too much drama?

Don't worry, I will write about the events of the party. You lovely readers have my word. But I have some exciting news to tell you all!'

Another horrific night, another dollar gained for the endless cycle of money, continues. A yawn overtook me, each bone in my body aching for respite after the gruelling night. I carried the last of the trash bags outback, my feet landing one after the other. Each lift of a trash bag sent spasms of soreness through my arms during the night. My whole being yearned for the soft embrace of my bed, a refuge from the physical toll.

"Just throw that out and be on your way, all right, Valeria!" I heard my manager call out.

I lugged the trash bags out the door with a last heave. "Got it!"

I opened the bin lid, grasped the black plastic, swung it in the air to gain momentum, and threw it in. It landed with a loud thud. I did the same with the other one and closed the black lid. The odour from the trash bin clawed at my nostrils, forcing me to hold my breath.

I shivered as the chilly wind blew through the alley, freezing my skin and bones. My teeth clacked together as the cold bit through me. I rushed to the door but froze as I heard a faint noise. Searching through this dark and empty alley, I could see the back lights and the streetlights on the other end. Providing enough light to see the brickwork of the tall buildings between.

I shook my head, attributing the noise to fatigue-fuelled imagination. I heard it again. It was clearer, but I couldn't tell where it was coming from. I walked closer to the darkness. The noise was louder, a high squeak. It wasn't a mouse, and recognition surged through me. My heart broke in two as my eyes landed on a broken, wet, old boot. It squeaked again. Its beautiful blue orbs stared back at me, begging to be picked up.

“Oh, sweety,” I cried. I could feel my eyes water at the sight. I knelt, creeping my hand closer to its nose. It sniffed and hopped out of the boot. Its golden and brown spotted fur was all wet. The poor thing shivered as it walked closer to my legs, seeking comfort. It was at that moment I felt my heart implode. Picking the little kitten up; it squeaked at me again and curled into my palms. Seeking warmth, it refused to jump out of them. I smiled at the damp fluff. “You’re coming home with me.”

It’s no secret that I am a cat person. I like dogs as well, but they have a lot of energy and need a lot of attention. Cats are mellow and to see an animal that needs help. I need to help them.

I carried the wrapped kitten in my arms, using my apron to shield it from the world and its cruel weather. As I made my journey home, along the way, the little ball of fluff fell asleep. I felt unease bringing this little creature into a den of vampires. It wasn't the fact that they would eat it. No, animal blood made them sick if they drank it over a long period. A knot of apprehension tightened in my stomach, fearing the words that might banish this little creature from my life.

I had a few tricks up my sleeve to convince them otherwise. But animals were known to fear vampires. They were predators, and animals could sense them. It would be cruel if the kitten was always on edge, but it might adjust since it was so young.

The elevator dinged its arrival, revealing the dimly lit hallway that always seemed to leer menacingly at me. My throat felt dry as I stepped out.

It was now or never.

Walking to the oak door, I let myself in and remembered wet shoes weren't allowed in the apartment. Nathaniel sat in the usual blue armchair, reading a book. His eyes shifted from the manuscript to me. He gave a wide grin, but then frowned, noticing the kitten in my arms. Nathaniel was before me, inspecting the little creature wrapped in my apron.

"Is that–a kitten?" he asked, sniffing it as well.

Okay, that's not weird.

'I have learnt some–trigger words? Is that how I should call it? Living with vampires, I learn they are loyal to each other. Willing to die or kill for one another, they are suckers for the word family or needing a family. Not something I advise to humans when encountering a vampire, but from one vampire to another vampire, I highly recommend.'

I unwrapped the damp kitten from my apron. Thankfully, it was a little drier than when I found it.

"He's all alone and needs a family." Nathaniel's eyes sprang wide open, and his mouth hung. I could see the convulsion in his eyes, lips moving in silence, hesitating to speak. He took a deep breath in, still eyeing the kitten, watching the little one staring back at him.

"Ask Brooklyn," his voice cracked. I smiled and headed out to the balcony. I had won the first battle. The second battle would be even more challenging. Brooklyn had always favoured dogs, but they never returned the sentiment, growling or skittering away at his presence. I slid the door open and shivered, wrapping the kitten around my arms and bringing it closer to my chest. The vampire was dozing off in his hammock, hands behind his head, his eyes closed with a dazed smile, ready to embrace the land of nod. Smiling, I skipped to the vampire.

One of his eyes opened and acknowledged my approach. "Welcome home." he yawned and opened both eyes. He frowned, still groggy. "Is that a kitten?" he asked, squinting at the little creature in my arms.

"He needs a family, and he is all alone. Nathaniel told me to ask you," I put the kitten on Brooklyn. He stiffened as the tiny, damp fluff ball was on his broad chest.

They stared at each other. The kitten purred and stared into Brooklyn's soul, and Brooklyn stared back like a deer in headlights. I saw him crack. His eyes softened, the stern facade crumbling under the tiny kitten's stare. "Some ground rules." Brooklyn cleared his throat and picked the kitten up off his chest, handing it back to me. "You feed it, look after it, vaccinate it, and take him to the vet tomorrow, and then you may keep it, understood?" Brooklyn demanded, as any father would say to their child who is asking for a pet.

"Yes! Thank you, thank you!" I squealed, rushing inside to tell Nathaniel the excellent news.

'Gosh, they're softies when they hear those words, string together in a sentence.'

Brooklyn agreed to come with me to the vet the following morning. It was busy. All the dogs were frenzied as he stepped into the reception. Their owners had to hold on to their leashes as their dogs charged at Brooklyn. Most apologised, and another responded, "He's not like this."

All of them barked at the vampire, and the humans were unaware of the predator in the room. Brooklyn had to excuse himself back outside, but made sure I would be all right by myself.

'Poor Brooklyn, he just wants to pat dogs.'

"So it's a boy," Brooklyn confirmed on the walk back home. I nodded, weaving around the mass crowds of people on the side street. Cars with loud engines drove past while the wind blew through the streets, making noise around tall buildings and covering the sun with clouds. My coat provided little protection.

"Y-yeah," my teeth chattered.

Brooklyn noticed and took off his own coat, putting it on me.

"Can't believe how expensive it is to vaccinate him. Will you be all right?" Brooklyn asked, looking at the vet bill in disbelief. Understanding what he meant, I gave him a reassuring smile.

"Yep, I'll just work longer shifts," I assured him. "Besides, I'd rather he's healthy and up to date with his vaccines, no matter the cost."

Brooklyn sighed. “All right. But he will need a name.”

“I’ve already decided.” There was a long pause before Brooklyn spoke up again.

“And that is?”

“Atem.”

'Yeah, yeah, I’m cheesy, I know. He was my first anime crush, I’ll admit. He was just so cool!'

Blog 23

Date: July 8th
Time 9AM

'Life adjusting to a kitten has been most amusing. I've given treats to the vampires, hoping Atem can associate positive emotions towards the creatures.

My logic to how the situation should play out.

'The vampire has food. Vampires give me food. I won't hiss at them.' This is what I think the cat would say.

Though I came across something that I would never have expected.'

My eyes were bleary as I fumbled with the keys and the late evening of the night wrapping me in an icy embrace. Each step inside felt like lifting a weight, a sigh escaping my lips. But as I thought of the overtime pay, a reluctant smile tugged at the corners of my mouth.

Oddly, Atem didn't greet me like he usually did whenever I came home.

I glanced around the apartment, but he wasn't in the kitchen. Nothing in the lounge, and the dining table and chairs were empty too. Suddenly, the sound of paws thumping and bouncing on the hardwood floors filled the silent space, followed by a hearty chuckle. It piqued my interest. I sneaked to my bedroom door, missing the squeaky floorboards.

There was Neil, with a stick and feather, playing with my little kitten in my room. I couldn't tear my eyes away as Atem's lithe form danced and pounced, each movement executed with feline grace. Atem was close to the floor, wiggling his back body as he pounced on the teasing feather. Neil laughed at his feeble attempts, patting Atem whenever he managed to catch the feather. The corners of Neil's mouth lifted, transforming his entire face. It was a look I hadn't seen before.

"Good job," Neil attempted to pet the kitten, but it attacked his hand. Neil snorted and picked Atem up, holding him like a baby. "You almost got 'em," he scratched Atem's belly. Atem stayed in Neil's arms, enjoying the belly scratches.

I felt a strange warmth in my chest, as if I were both flying and sinking at the same time. Our eyes met, and the smile vanished from Neil's face, replaced by a tense grimace as he suddenly looked away. He pulled himself up from the floor, cleared his throat, and opened the door wider. He handed the kitten back to me.

"Never mention this to anyone," he hissed and left Atem and me alone.

'Well, that didn't last long. At least he didn't try to kill me again, so that's a plus.'

"Atem, here, kitty," I called out, making kissing noises.

It is the second month, and he needed his flea treatment. I live in an apartment. What are the odds? It's not the odds that he'll get fleas from the apartment. It's the odd chance of encountering another cat with fleas. I don't want to take the risk.

I glanced over at Nathaniel, who was still reading the same novel on the night I brought Atem home. He grasped the delicate handle of a fine china teacup and sipped from it while engrossed in his book. The beautiful blue artwork on the cup complemented the white ceramic.

The most British man to ever British.

"You haven't seen Atem, have you?" I asked Nathaniel's eyes remained glued to his book, the furrow between his brows deepening as he huffed

Ah, he was in one of those moods.

"No," he replied and put the teacup down on its saucer. "But ask Brooklyn. Maybe he's seen the little scamp," he added before returning to his book. Slumping my shoulders, I headed outside to the balcony. The sun felt pleasantly warm on my skin; I could understand why cats enjoy sleeping in the warm beam of light.

Brooklyn was shirtless, tending to the garden. I glanced over to the clothesline, watching it sway in the wind, and noticing droplets of water falling to the ground. Brooklyn hoisted the large bags of soil with ease, making me marvel at his effortless strength.

“Hey, Brooklyn, have you seen Atem?” I asked.

“Nope, ask Neil maybe,” he shrugged, trimming away at the hedge.

I retreated inside, my eyes fixed on Neil’s bedroom door, noticing a tiny gap underneath. He always shut it, no matter the occasion. I grasped the doorknob and pushed on the oak. Out of all the rooms, Neil’s was the only one I hadn’t seen. It was nothing exciting–plain blue walls, a white cream carpet, and a bed in the back.

Neil was asleep, and Atem was sleeping soundly on his chest, curled up into a little ball. A bitter taste rising in my mouth as I stared at the cozy scene. A pang shot through me as Atem nuzzled Neil. Why him? I thought, my grip tightening on the doorknob. Introducing the kitten to Neil turned out to be better than I expected.

'Kittens, they can turn any sociopathic vampire into a softie.'

Blog 24

Time: July 14th
Time: 2PM

'I notice how many readers I have overseas and realised some of you may not know our slang or our weather. School is different here compared to many places.

So I gave an educational post on us Aussies. Don't worry, Brooklyn had to ask too.'

"Can you help me with something?" Brooklyn asked, charging into my room with a laptop in hand and plopping himself onto my bed. Thankfully, he didn't sit on Atem. With an audible exhale, my shoulders dropped as I expelled my frustration in a single breath.

“No, please, come in. Like, I had nothing to do,” I groaned. My eyes darted between Brooklyn and the open textbooks and laptop screen in front of me, scattered with multiple tabs and a blinking cursor.

“It’s important!” he urged. I rolled my eyes, saved my work, pushed my seat back, and rose to put on my orange slippers. They squeaked against the wooden floorboards with each step. As I sat beside him, our arms brushed, sending an unexpected shiver down my spine, each hair standing on end.

“What seems to be the problem?” I asked, and he handed the laptop over.

“What does this mean?” he asked, and I looked at the screen, suppressing my urge to laugh. Brooklyn had his own social media account! He was one step ahead of Nathaniel. Every time social media was mentioned,

Nathaniel would scrunch his nose as if he'd smelled something bad, firmly asserting his disdain. I looked at the message blinking in the corner of his screen.

'portable garden beds.'

Oh, Brooklyn.

My eyes scanned the text on the screen, absorbing each word with a blend of amusement and disbelief.

'Oh yeah, Nah mate, whatcha gotta do is chuck a U-ey when you pass Maccas. When you see the servo, go left and dead set. I'll be at the end of the street. I won't be home till the arvo, though, but you won't find anything with better quality. So many people do a dodgy.'

"He's giving you directions to do a U-turn when you see McDonald's, then when you see the service station, go left, and at the end of the street. He will be there until this afternoon. He also says people try to scam you by selling you poor quality," As I finished decoding the message, Brooklyn stared at me, his jaw slackening in apparent astonishment.

"How do you understand that?" he gawked, grabbing the laptop back from me and re-reading the text.

"I'm an Aussie. How else?" I replied with a shrug. The laptop dinged, and another message appeared.

'You seem like an all right bloke. I'll give it to you for some tinnies.' Brooklyn looked at me again.

"Beer, he wants a beer."

“I was planning on eating him and then taking the garden beds,” Brooklyn shrugged and leaned back, arms crossed. An eerie sense of nonchalance in his voice as he discussed his meal plans alongside his gardening ones. “Please tell me you are discreet about this?” My eyes widened, voice tinged with apprehension, as I considered the risks of his online adventures

“I am, I am. Look, that’s not even my real name,” He nodded, reassuring me with an earnest stare and a pointed finger toward the screen. “And I delete the account after every meal. No one can find me.” The corners of his mouth stretched wider, exposing his fangs in a grin that radiated self-satisfaction

“And deleting the messages on their accounts, hiding your IP address,” My brows furrowed, as I tacked on other considerations of digital stealth, waiting to see if he'd grasp the seriousness of it.

"Maybe." His eyes flickered with uncertainty, his response trailing off, clearly not fully comprehending the implications of my words.

"Please stick to the old-fashioned way."

'So that's my fun story, but here are some other words:

Sick day–sicky

French fries, crisps, chips–all referred to as chips.

Mosquito–mozzie

Cry Baby–sook

Cooler–esky.

Yeah, we like to shorten a lot of words. We're pretty laid back.

Have any of you lovely readers visited Australia? And what were your thoughts?'

I watched Brooklyn deftly swipe through his phone, remembering the days when he used to jab frustratingly at the screen. Unsure of how it worked until I had guided him on how to be a millennial. Nathaniel, though, had resisted. Each time I reached out to take Nathaniel's phone to assist him, he had pulled it back as if guarding a treasure. I had averted my eyes as Nathaniel tried to figure out how to use a smartphone, unable to keep my grimace hidden. He had refused to understand the basics of the power button and then tried to jam the charger into the headphone jack.

Plz stahp.

In the events that had led up to this, I didn't know where Nathaniel had gotten it. I had come home one night, and there he had been in the kitchen; on top of the black granite countertop lay a package. Unwrapped, cardboard torn apart, paper unwrapped, and bubble wrap—lots and lots of bubbles wrap. My fingers had hovered over the plastic-filled bubbles. My fingers itched, twitching with the desire to pop the air out of the plastic.

The bubble wrap had needed to be popped. I had needed the bubble wrap.

So there I had been on a Sunday morning, sitting on the lounge popping the stash of bubble wrap I had stolen a few nights earlier, watching Nathaniel try to work out the phone. Neil had lain on the other lounge, using his phone with ease, and Atem had curled up on my lap, asleep. Brooklyn had been nowhere to be seen inside. Nathaniel had glanced out the window at the gathering clouds, his eyes narrowing, calculating the minutes Brooklyn had left outside. With every pop, I noticed Nathaniel's grip had tightened on his phone, his jaw clenched in mounting frustration.

'pop.'

Nathaniel had flinched again.

'pop.'

Again.

'pop.'

"Will you stop that infernal popping!" Nathaniel screamed, losing his cool. Atem jumped at Nathaniel's sudden outburst, and Neil looked away from his phone, glaring at Nathaniel. He had scared his favourite kitten. There would be hell to pay.

"Then give me the goddamn phone!" I hissed, and my hands slammed onto the armrest. Frustration had bubbled over. "You've been at it for a day and refuse to let anyone help you!" I complained, clenching my teeth. Atem settled himself again and went back to sleep on my lap. Atem purred as I stroked him, and my anger diffused with each pat. Nathaniel raked his fingers through his hair, tidying the loose strands away. He sighed, dragging his feet, and handed the phone over to me.

"Can you—please—help?" he asked through clenched teeth, swallowing his pride. Neil snorted, not making the situation any better. "How—do you turn it on?" Nathaniel asked.

"Is it charged?" I asked him, and Nathaniel's face went blank as if I had spoken another language. I sighed.

This was going to be a long day.

Blog 25 – Part 1

Date: Aug 10th
Time: 5am

‘I thought living with vampires would be the strangest thing I’ve been writing in my blog, but this isn’t the case. Not only are there vampires and werewolves, there is a whole supernatural order, and I have only just scratched the surface. The most bizarre piece of information will be in this post and... I hope some of you believe me.’

Tonight was the night. I took in my appearance. I created a small bun by neatly tying my medium-length brown hair. Pale white skin complemented the black and red dress Nathaniel and I had picked out together. My green eyes shone like luminescent seaweed on a sunny day. Red heels gave me a few more centimetres in height; if I were to stand next to Brooklyn, I would meet his shoulder. In the mirror, the dress seemed to betray me—emphasising a rounded stomach, tugging tight against my arms, and drawing attention to an unintentional slouch. My heart drummed against my ribcage while a hot wave cascaded down my spine. Thoughts raced uncontrollably, tripping over each other.

Is my tummy too big? Am I overdressed? Will they see me as dinner? Is this my last night home? Am I going to be the laughingstock of the party? Will werewolves crash the party?

An icy hand grasped my shoulder, and yanked me back to reality, as if they pulled me out of frigid water.

My panicked mind snapped to attention, and I swung around, stilling like a cornered wild animal.

“Woah,” Brooklyn’s hands shot up, his eyes wide before me. “Your heart is beating like crazy. Are you all right?” he asked. A deep breath wobbled on its way in, bumping against the sudden lump in my throat and stirring a nervous flutter in my stomach.

“Yeah–just nervous.” I tried to swallow my anxiety. I gave myself one last look over. “Is - is everyone else ready?” I asked, looking at his reflection. The vampire cleaned up nicely. A black tailored vest, matching his slacks, a simple buttoned white shirt, his beard clean from dirt and twigs, his hair gelled, spiking upwards.

“They are,” he answered, and I looked back up at him.

Shit, have I been holding everyone up?

Brooklyn's hands settled on my shoulders, grounding me while my mind felt like a ship in a thunderstorm. “It’s okay,” he assured me. “Breathe, remember to breathe.” I nodded my head, taking deep breaths in and out. “I just came in to give you something,” he said.

Brooklyn reached for the back pocket of his black dress pants and held out a sheathed knife. I watched in awe as he unsheathed the blade. Old steel, glistening polish, shining in the dim light, the blade sharp and deadly, hadn’t tasted blood since the world war. An illegal ivory handle, firmly gripped in his hand, and the brown leather pouch for the blade’s bed.

“Brooklyn,” my voice was but a whisper. Brooklyn pursed his lips together, sheathing the blade, grasping my hand with his cold one, and putting the knife in my hand.

"I can't promise your safety when we get there, but if the opportunity presents itself, I need you to fight back. All right?" he asked me. I nodded, staring at the knife in my hand.

'*I know the perfect place to hide it.*'

"When did you get this?" I asked him, and Brooklyn gave me a sad smile.

"It was my old hunting knife back in the war. She got me out of a lot of sticky situations, saved my life even. It's yours." My chest felt tight, my eyes watered.

"Thank you," my voice cracked a little. Brooklyn chuckled a little and wrapped me in a hug.

"You're all right," he soothed.

"Any second longer, and I'll have to bleach my eyes," I recognised the snarky voice from behind. Brooklyn let me go, and I saw Neil standing in the doorway. Neil's scowl looked as if they had carved it so deep and unyielding they were permanent lines around his mouth. How unfortunate it's ruining his attractive ensemble. It completed his outfit with a dark red dress shirt, a black tie, and his favourite pair of black dress pants and shoes. Simple.

"Figures for anyone to ruin a delicate moment. It'd be you," I scoffed. Neil only rolled his eyes.

"Yeah, and we've been waiting for you and Brooklyn for the last five minutes," he hissed. We both sighed at Neil and followed behind him. Nathaniel proudly stood tall in the living room. His eyes sparkled as if hiding a delightful secret, while his foot tapped an impatient dance on the floor. Nathaniel looked debonair in his white traditional tux, perfectly complementing his tanned skin. He dressed as if he was going to the Opera.

"Right!" Nathaniel chirped. "Let's get going."

'It was an emotional experience between Brooklyn and I. it completely took aback me when he handed me his knife. But the evening had an even more remarkable moment. It gets better.'

"Nathaniel, are you sure you're reading the directions, right?" I asked as we wandered through the streets. The sun had just set, and the night was coming to life. Restaurants and takeaways opened up, releasing the delicious smell of cooked meats and seasoned side dishes. My stomach grumbled, its echoing demand for food almost a separate entity within me. Neil snorted, snickering at my bodily functions.

"This is the right place," Nathaniel snapped, turning to me and waving his phone in front of my face. I looked at the rundown building before us. An old apartment block, decorated in vulgar graffiti, smashed windows, broken doors, and a large sign showing development to happen soon.

"May I?" I put my hand out, asking for his phone. Nathaniel was hesitant to hand over the device, but he gave in. I looked at the address. My brow furrowed as I wracked my brain over the city's layout. None of this was making sense. "Nathaniel, this place doesn't exist." Nathaniel's eyes widened, ripping the phone from my hands and looking at the address with trembling hands.

"What! He gave me this phone and said it will lead me there," he blurted and turned to incoherent rambling. Neil sighed and took the phone out of Nathaniel's hands. He read over the address and sighed once more.

"It's still leading us to the right location," Neil clarified. Nathaniel ranted on, unconvinced and uninterested. "They permeate the phone with magic. Of course, the party is there," he grumbled and put the phone in his pocket. Neil walked over to the abandoned building, his hand trailing across the concrete, searching amongst the rubble. We approached the cracked window, our reflections looking back at us. Our curious eyes met in the reflection on the glass as we waited and watched Neil trace his finger in a specific pattern. The light seemed to drain from Neil's eyes, leaving them dull as he stared at the glass. A shaky breath escaped his throat, and he swallowed down the emotion that threatened to break him. “He knew I would be coming. That’s why he chose a different world,” he deadpanned.

“I’m sorry?” Nathaniel blurted. “But what?” he snapped. Marching towards the young vampire, he glanced over his shoulder and saw nothing but his own reflection.

“You can’t see it because you don’t have ‘The Sight’,” he murmured, drawing his hand away and leaning closer to the smashed window. “Aperio,” he commanded.

The window disappeared, and a rectangular box opened before us. An alley opened up, leading down its mouth to bright city lights, the sounds of people laughing and talking. The eldest vampires peered down the open door, Nathaniel’s mouth left hanging open while

Brooklyn watched. Without another word, Neil stepped through. Brooklyn was hesitant, but he followed. Nathaniel sighed as he saw the other two get through and walked across. With a gulp that did little to dislodge the lump in my throat, I took the last step through the gateway. I let out a breath of relief.

Neil walked back and whispered one word. "Claudere." The door closed, returning to a brick wall.

Latin. Of course, it's fucking Latin.

"How?" My whisper barely broke the silence, my eyes searching Neil's for some kind of explanation. He looked back at the other two vampires, his lips pursed, and fished for the phone.

"It's a door," he replied simply. "Vampires and magiqs use it to world jump. You could even use it to visit locations within the world you are staying in and visit other places," he explained.

"You have a lot of explaining to do." Brooklyn hissed.

"Do you realise how much money I could save? I wouldn't have to fly. I could be in Europe for lunch and be home for bed. It's every anxious person's dream!" My words bubbled out, accelerated by a surge of exhilarating possibilities coursing through my veins "Like they don't have to experience gruelling twenty-three-hour flights, where they are away from their comfort zone and not have a panic attack before the flight and refusing to get on and losing all their money," I blabbed on, and Neil looked at me.

"It sounds like it happened to you."

"Maybe," I shrugged, playing it cool.

'It did. I was meant to go to Europe for a month on a Contiki tour. I had a panic attack and refused to get on the plane. I don't regret missing out, but I regret losing all the money.'

Blog 26 – part 2

Date: Aug 10th
Time: 9AM

"Should I leave you and the building alone for a minute?" Neil's voice rang as he flashed a white smile at me.

"Well, if you don't mind, I'm sure this building would be more preferable company than you," I sassed. Neil's smile disappeared, his eyes narrowing to a sharp glare. We faced off at each other, refusing to look away, refusing to blink.

"Jeez, get a room, you two," Brooklyn interjected, walking between us and ruining the standoff. Nathaniel did the same with a broad smile. Neil said nothing, but he looked less menacing than before. I huffed and followed Brooklyn's lead. Neil trailed behind.

The building was an enormous structure that put all the other skyscrapers to shame. Glass covered every square meter, creating a reflective shell that, at the right angle of the sun, could set a building on fire.

Inside, it looked normal. I expected something dramatic, like nineteenth-century gothic furnishings or everything draped in black. Instead, met with beautiful blue marble floors and white marble walls mixed with obsidian, creating natural swirls and patterns. No human could replicate a design like this. Dark Italian leather lounges were at the far end of the lobby, with an elegant oak coffee table centring on the arrangement. The reception area was dark and empty, and the stainless steel elevators were quiet and inactive. Even standing with three other vampires, a shiver crawled up my spine, the empty air seeming to press in around me. Neil took the phone he had confiscated from Nathaniel out of his pocket. The phone unlocked, its sound echoing in the quiet lobby. I sought comfort leaning closer to Brooklyn, expecting something to jump out from the shadows. Neil handed the phone back to Nathaniel and headed to the fourth elevator, his footsteps echoing in the empty lobby.

"This building is a headquarters for travelling vampires. A place to stay, meet up, hold parties, or meetings," Neil explained, turning to us with a grim look.

"How do you know so much?" Brooklyn asked again, standing over the young vampire. His chest puffed out as he gave Neil a sharp glare. The elevator signalled its arrival, its doors opening for us to enter.

"One day I will explain," Neil said, looking away from the vampire's harsh glare. "Shall we?" He turned away and stepped inside. Brooklyn clenched his jaw and exhaled, as if stowing away a grudge for another time. Nathaniel and I soon followed suit, and the doors enclosed us.

Trying to focus on the present moment, I concentrated on my breathing.

I'm going to get eaten. I'm going to die. This is my last moment. This is it!

An icy hand grasped my own, snapping me back to reality. I looked at the hand attached to it, and it was Neil's. He kept his face forward, refusing to make eye contact, but he squeezed my hand for reassurance. A fluttering sensation filled my chest as warmth crept into my cheeks. Such a slight gesture had such a significant impact.

The elevator signalled the end of the ride. Neil let go of my hand, and the doors opened up. The experience failed to meet my expectations again. I had expected something more dramatic, more goth interior, blood spilled on the floor, and humans lying dead. But, no, instead, it was a normal, modern design.

The entire top floor unfurled as an expansive open area. To the left, a bar exuded the rich scent of aged whiskey and fresh citrus garnishes. To the right, a glass-panelled balcony offered sweeping vistas of the twinkling cityscape below, the distant hum of traffic and laughter wafting up to us.

The walls, crafted from white marble, boasted organic swirls of light blue, creating an ethereal atmosphere. As I stepped onto the hardwood floor, my heels clack against the polished wood. Suspended above, a crystal chandelier shimmered, its intricate facets refracting light in a dazzling dance—its antique charm contrasting sharply with the modern elegance surrounding it.

This event, gathering, or whatever you want to call it, was unusual by human standards, but by vampire standards, it was very normal. Everyone dressed as they felt comfortable. Some wore casual clothing, some formal, and some in between. At least I didn't stand out as I predicted. This put me more at ease. Everyone seemed to have their own niche, a group to hang around with until the end of the night. My easiness dissipated, and already I wanted to go back in the elevator and find a quiet place to hide. I didn't like parties, especially parties with lots of people or vampires I didn't know. I had the social skills of a lamppost. Awkward. I wanted to go home.

Nathaniel abandoned us and dragged Brooklyn with him, wishing to greet the host for this evening. Much to Brooklyn's protest, Neil wandered off to the bar, and they left me standing alone, well off to the side, trying to hide.

"Well now," I stiffened, feeling the cold air tickling the back of my neck. "I didn't expect to welcome a new family member!" the strange vampire grinned, slapping a hand over my shoulder.

Family member?!

The vampire's bright red eyes pierced through me as he gave a fanged smile. His short, dark brown hair swept to one side as he raked his fingers through it.

I'm dead.

"U-Um, I-I'm so- what?" I stumbled over my words, and the vampire laughed.

"Relax!" he chuckled. "We're not gonna eat you," he grinned.

We?

"Shade!" we both directed our attention forward. A young woman, far younger than me.

She was the most underdressed out of everyone in the room, and she couldn't care less. Wearing a white tank top to show off her tattoos, black skinnies, and combat boots. Her hair kept to the left and shaved on the sides around the scalp. She was a tad shorter, but she stood tall before us. Her piercing hazel eyes stared into Shade's. Her arms crossed, and red fiery tattoos wrapped around her skin up to her elbows. The markings represented a Phoenix on each arm and gave off a faint glow.

"Ceres!" Shade greeted the other human. "I was just about to show our new member around!" He pushed me forward toward Ceres. She raised an eyebrow at me. Next to her towering presence, I felt like a pebble beside a mountain.

"Oh no, you're not getting out of this," she hissed at the vampire. "Hiding behind some abeyant under the pretence of 'showing them around'."

"How can you be so mean!" Shade cried, his hand on his chest. Ceres's eyes hardened and flashed vibrant red, I was so used to seeing. Her lips turned into a scowl, showing off her fangs to Shade. I stood between them, as if I didn't exist.

"Ah, Valeria!" we all directed our attention to the voice that called my name. I recognised the long brown curly hair anywhere.

"Bellamy," Ceres hissed. "Where's your fan club, not allowed in?" she smirked. Her red eyes disappeared and returned to their normal hazel.

"Unfortunately, you are correct. This is official business and all," Bellamy pouted, and Ceres could only roll her eyes.

"Odd. I thought you would need them to stroke your ego for the bullshit that comes out of your mouth," Ceres smirked.

"You certainly know how to wound me," he mocked, taking a step forward to Ceres. Eyes locked and silently daring the other to make the first move.

"Oh, I can wound you a lot more if I want to," Ceres threatened, clenching her fists, the markings pulsating as she did. A wave of warmth radiated from her clenched fists, as though she held captive embers. Bellamy's eyes followed down to her fists, monitoring them.

"Ok!" Shade stepped in. "Ceres, I hear Zack is calling for you. Let's go find him," Shade tried to push Ceres away. She gave one final growl to Bellamy before finally moving.

"C'mon you idiot, let's go find the others," she murmured and left me alone with Bellamy.

"Well now," Bellamy's voice pierced through my daze, pulling me back to the room. "Would you like a drink?"

Blog 27–part 3

Date: Aug 10
Time 11AM

Bellamy's throat emitted a low, intentional hum, and his lips curled into a smile.

"I'm glad you could make it." He beamed. "I'm rather pleased to see my plan worked," Bellamy praised, his eyes twinkled with self-satisfaction, as if he had just solved a complex puzzle.

"Plan?" I asked, raising my brow in question, and the vampire's smile didn't break. He placed his chilly hand on my back with care and directed me to the balcony outside.

"For Neil to take the bait, I knew he would come along if I invited you," Bellamy revealed. "It's been twenty years since I've seen Neil care about something again. No hard feelings, I hope," he said with an afterthought and shrugged. I squinted at the vampire, my mind churning through the pieces of the puzzle he'd just laid out. Bellamy's eyes darted to mine, picking up on my bewilderment before a soft snicker escaped his lips. "I wouldn't threaten someone who is part of the family," he continued. "I had to be sure. If he did nothing when I threatened your existence, well then, back to the drawing board. But he stepped in, and that is when I knew I had my link."

"Gee, thanks," I sneered, and Bellamy laughed. "But why go to so much effort for him? Couldn't it be any other vampire?" I asked, shooting a stony stare. "What's your motive?" I hissed. Bellamy's face remained a serene landscape, as if he had expected my barrage of questions all along. He just kept smiling like the sweet gentleman he pretended to be.

"Nothing sinister, I assure you, just want the little vampire to take his role back, that's all," Bellamy shrugged.

Role? What role?

"Ah well. Small steps. Once you've turned, maybe things will be easier."

"I'm sorry, what?"

"They haven't told you?" he asked. I shook my head, growing even more frustrated. "You're one of us." For a second, I felt my heart stop. The world turned calm and stiff as wind blew through me, like a hollow tree. Bellamy put his hand to his mouth, his brow furrowing while doing so. "Hmm, I suppose they don't know either. Neil's last lesson was to pick up the scent of

Abeyant. It's a shame, his sire-." He cut himself off. A cheeky grin replaced his stern expression.

"Ah, maybe I shouldn't say anymore. It is quite a sensitive topic," he mused. "But maybe if you get the young vampire to open up, he might tell you." Bellamy smiled like the Cheshire cat. My eyes narrowed, scepticism clouding my gaze as I pondered his veiled intentions. Bellamy gave a hearty laugh. Before I opened my mouth again, we cut our conversation short.

"Bellamy!" Our attention snapped to Neil. His fangs bared at the older vampire, who flashed a brilliant smile at Neil.

"I don't think Neil wants to hug him.

Neil stormed up to the vampire, staring him down with each step. Bellamy didn't back down. He only put his arms down and continued to smile at Neil until their noses were inches away from each other.

"Stay away from her," Neil hissed.

"Oh?" Bellamy quipped. "I thought you didn't care about her?" he questioned the other vampire.

Neil only smiled, his canines still bared.

"I don't. I just want you to keep your mouth shut," Neil hissed. Bellamy continued to smile and shrugged it off.

"Oh, don't worry, my mouth is sealed. I just gave enough to spark a flame." Bellamy dismissed Neil, their shoulders just touching as Bellamy walked inside. Neil walked up to the railing and slumped his arms on the glass pane and sighed.

"What did he say?" he asked me. I shifted my arms onto the railing, matching Neil's posture.

"A few things," I answered, and Neil remained stoic.

"Such as?"

"I'm meant to be a vampire, and that he wants you to take back your role." Neil's jaw tightened, and he seemed to be searching for answers—or maybe an escape—in the sprawling cityscape below

"Not surprised he told you," he said. "All this work just to get to me," he whispered. "Bellamy is nothing but a thorn in my side," His eyes burned with an intensity that, if focused, seemed like it could ignite the very skyline.

"Care to explain what an Abeyant is?" I asked. "This is the second time tonight I have been called that."

"Abeyant. The word means inactive, suspended for a time," he explained. "We use this word to describe humans who are waiting to be turned. Waiting to become like us. Your very soul begs for it, and it's how we figure out who is meant to be a vampire and who isn't."

"So much complications just to become a vampire," I shrugged.

"When you live in a multiverse with other variants of you running around," he said. "You gotta have a system in place."

"They couldn't make it simple, could they?" I said with a smile.

"Nope. There are a few ways, but smell is the easiest one," he shrugged. The vampire straightened himself and looked at me.

"If you never told Nathaniel you were alone, I wouldn't have attacked."

"So what? You had a choice not to, just like them, but you acted," I called him out. "Are you afraid?" Neil snapped his head at me, his glower unable to touch me. I remained calm, waiting for his reply as the noise of the party inside kept us company. "Why are you like this?" I hissed. Neil bared his canines at me. He took a step forward and leaned to my ear.

"I'm fucking terrified," he whispered. A crack, a small crack, but it's a crack in the armour. Neil took a deep breath. "I want to snuff out any feelings you stirred," he snarled. "I don't want to get close. Never do I want to experience that again." his breath was icy, but his words burned through me. "But I couldn't touch you. Not if there was a chance of us getting caught, risking our safety," he whispered through clenched teeth. "I hate you for coming into my life and changing me," he hissed and drew back from my ear. His emotions and face conflicted with each other. I could see the pain and hurt swirling in his eyes as he kept his muscles steady, unmoving, blank like a canvas, his face set in complete stone. I remembered Brooklyn's words echoing in my head.

'Valeria turns up, and years of work I have put in - she puts the cracks in his armour in only four months. He's changed so much since she's been here, and he knows that's why Valeria terrifies him.'

I grasped Neil's hand. He didn't move nor flinch as I held his icy hand in mine.

"That night was the first night you said something nice to me, and that terrified you, didn't it?" I asked him. I knew he wanted to answer, but silence was enough. My head dipped in a slow nod, the weight of my decision settling over me. “You’re terrified, I get that. But I need to know what caused it.” I gave him half a smile. “So let’s make a deal.”

“A deal,” Neil's voice wavered for a moment, as if he was on the edge of an emotional cliff.

“Tell me the cause of your fear, and I’ll leave. You will never have to worry about me again. Savy?” I asked him, posing like a pirate as I made the agreement. Neil scrunched his nose, frustrated. To be pinned to the corner, he would get rid of the one thing he cares for and goes back to his life of solitude.

A heavy sigh escaped Neil, and his hand clamped around mine as if cementing a pact.

“It’s a deal.”

'The event overall was fun, but it became serious, really quickly'

"So far, the werewolves had begun taking over the other city," Ceres began. "Along with its variants in the other worlds."

Two vampires brought a large table into the centre of the ballroom. It reminded me of a tabletop, little figures sitting in certain locations on the map, moving all around, showing the infiltrated areas. "They have started to make their move here." Ceres moved the werewolf figure across the river. "If we let them take hold of the others, they will soon start moving into Sydney and then Brisbane."

"How do you suggest we stop them?" Bellamy asked.

“Right at the root,” she answered. “The werewolves are mostly coming from the world with no Palatine, world Alteris.” An uncomfortable silence fell as multiple eyes landed on Neil. The young vampire shifted uncomfortably, his eyes darting away as if each stare was a physical weight upon him. He refused to look up from his shoes. “Cut the head off the snake and the rest will fall.”

“Are you sure?” A strange vampire asked.

“All the orders are coming from that world,” said Ceres. “I’m certain.”

‘My Home world hasn’t had a Palatine over the look the city in twenty years, resulting in the worst werewolf outbreak the vampire Coven is facing. There is so much for me to learn. I can’t imagine what's out there, and I'm itching to see it. But first, I have got to deal with Neil before I can set off into the vast unknown.'

Blog 28 – part 1

Date: 25th of August
Time 1:26PM

'Hoo boy, that was an interesting gathering, werewolf take over plots, social expectations, story reveals and the weekend has only just started.'

Brooklyn charged ahead, nearly running into a full sprint, already rehearsing the questions he'd fire at Neil. We didn't even cross the threshold before Brooklyn began his assault. Neil crossed his arms and looked away, ignoring Brooklyn's insistent questions. Brooklyn was well on his way to getting into a fistfight with Neil. Nathaniel had to step in and break them apart before they could destroy Nathaniel's precious furniture.

I waited for when Neil and I had peace to talk. A deal was a deal, and I wasn't leaving until I got my answer. It took a week before Neil approached me one afternoon on the balcony. Neil sat on the outdoor table set, leaning his arms on the table and watching me as I worked on my assignments. Nathaniel had business to attend to, and Brooklyn went hunting.

He cleared his throat, giving me a weak smile. I nodded, saved my assignment, and closed my laptop, waiting for the vampire to begin.

1964

At sixteen, Neil was tall but lacked much muscle and was a scrawny kid. Gangs would jump him, boys twice his age picking fights as he walked the streets late at night.

Why would a sixteen-year-old be alone at night, wandering the empty streets and picking fights? These were the moments Neil thrived on. To feel something other than the toxic numbness that had become well acquainted with him throughout the years. His fists clenched, and he gritted his teeth—yet another restless night. It was the reason he started looking for fights, provoking males by pretending to come on to them. It was the quickest reaction he could get.

The thrill of the fight, blood spilling, some fights he won unscathed or bloody and bruised, and some he lost. On the ground, coughing up his own blood, but he didn't care. Neil saw this as a step closer to death and would grow frustrated whenever he survived his injuries.

It was no secret he would prefer death over life, but something inside him, unexplainable and itching in the back of his head, told him it wasn't his time.

Time, time for what!? Neil often wondered.

Neil built quite a reputation for himself, starting fights, damaging property, petty theft. Officers would spot Neil lurking in the dark alleys, only to lose sight of him around the next corner or find their handcuffs mysteriously empty. Downtown was notorious for empty buildings, and they were a perfect place to hide in. Adults were on the lookout, the school was searching for him, and his parents were 'worried sick.'

"Local boy runs away, parents searching for him," the headlines would read.

Searching, huh? Yeah, right?

Neil slid his back against the brick wall, his butt hitting the hard concrete in the alley. He looked at both entrances and relaxed, knowing he was safe for now.

He could feel his own eyelids growing heavy, his breathing lightening, yawning following. His muscles ached with each step, and his breaths came in ragged gasps as he replayed the night's battles in his head. Everything just felt numb.

Darkness embraced him.

🩸🩸-----(＼(•̀ᵥᵥ•́)ノ)-----🩸🩸

Abrupt pain woke Neil from his slumber. He recognised a few of the youths who surrounded him, all screaming and shouting his name, dragging him to his feet. Neil kicked and punched those who dared to touch him. He even bared his teeth at them. Something told him it was a good idea.

They all laughed, and he managed to punch one of them in the gut.

“Well, well, well,” a voice echoed throughout the alley. The group’s cheers and laughter died down as the leader approached closer.

He grinned at Neil, moving in close to Neil’s face before striking him across the cheek. Neil’s cheek throbbed as he glared back at the leader. “Look what the cat dragged in,” the leader chuckled. “How’s it going, traitor?” he asked.

Neil only stared at the leader, furrowing his brow. Nothing was making sense.

“What, traitor? What the fuck are you talking about?” Neil hissed. The leader struck him across the face again.

“You,” the leader then grabbed a handful of Neil’s hair. “Telling my boys how to get in the warehouse,” he explained, his lips near Neil’s ear. “They’re dead because of you,” the leader growled, tightening his grip.

Neil remembered that night. He had been so proud to break into the impenetrable fortress downtown. No one knew who owned or lived in the warehouse, but no one had gotten in except Neil, and he knew how. “I told them how to get in. I didn’t expect them to die!” Neil screamed out. Clenching his teeth afterwards, he tried to deal with the pain.

“Yeah, well, now their blood is on your hands,” He lets go and snaps his fingers. “Bring him along.”

Neil tried to fight them the whole way, struggling to get out of their grip. They muffled his shout for help as a rough hand clamped over his mouth. Cold steel kissed the skin of his throat, silencing him further. As much as Neil wanted death, he wanted to go in his own way, not by the hands of some asshole.

A cold emptiness spread through Neil's chest, sinking rapidly into his gut as he faced the familiar building. It's the same warehouse he robbed a week ago.

"You're gonna go in there, and you gonna bring back the loot my boys promised," the leader snickered, and his gang laughed.

They removed the rag from his mouth, and Neil felt like he could breathe again.

"And what makes you think I wouldn't die in there?" Neil asked.

Their leader just shrugged. "I didn't, but it's a win-win either way."

They pushed Neil forward towards the large brick building. It was old, abandoned, or so they thought.

Someone had shattered the windows and covered them up with wooden planks.

Neil took a shaky breath and headed to the back of the building. He remembered one of the loose planks at the last window on the ground floor. He lifted the plank and moved it out of the way, sliding the gyprock to the left and slithering himself in. He put the plank back and the gyprock back in place. The room he stood in is an abyss. He could only hear his breathing and feel his heart beating in his chest.

Before he could turn around, they grabbed him from behind. Neil didn't scream.

Blog 29 – part 2

Date: August 25th
Time: 1:42PM

Neil was being dragged by his arms. Whatever had a grip on him was cold, hard, and unyielding. Neil felt each pulse thrum violently against his ribcage as he was pulled toward the dim glow. A single lamp hung from the roof, providing little light.

They threw him into the light, and he landed on all fours. His stare stayed locked on the uneven surface of the concrete floor, his whole body quivering uncontrollably.

Neil heard murmurs and whispers in the darkness. He couldn't see them, but he could hear them.

'He's just a kid.'

'How young do you think?'

'You think he's with them?'

Panic welled up inside Neil, cornered like a lamb, ready for the slaughter.

Neil heard clicking noises and then a light. He could see a cigarette being lit and listened to them blow out the smoke.

The room snapped and filled with light, allowing him to see his captors around him. Twenty people were in the room, all staring at him like some animal in a zoo. His eyes locked onto the figure, flicking the lighter.

A woman appeared to be in her early thirties. Her red lips held the cigarette in her mouth, her vibrant red eyes piercing into his soul. She took a drag and studied him, blowing out the puff of smoke and hummed in answer. Raking her fingers through her short sandy blonde hair, she shifted in her seat, crossing her legs.

"You're the stupidest kid I know or the bravest. Which one is it?" she broke the silence within the steel walls. Neil pursed his lips together and kept quiet. She smiled, showing off her long canines. "Don't want to talk, do ya? That's fine." She shrugged, getting up onto her feet. She stalked towards him, grasping the hair at the back of his neck. Neil gritted his jaw, bearing through the sharp pain. "Little punks like you always try to sneak in, take our stuff. There's a reason no one comes out alive," she hissed.

Neil couldn't help but stare at the long canines, threatening to inch closer to his neck. For years, he had denied the existence of these creatures, refusing to believe the stories on the street. He ignored them all and just kept moving, even if there was some evidence to back it up. Bodies drained of blood and inhuman-like teeth marks on their necks and arms.

She gave Neil a broad smile, licking her lips and baring her teeth closer to his neck. Neil could feel her icy breath tickling his skin, causing goosebumps to rise. His heart beat in his ears, and he felt a slight sting as the sharp edges of her fangs slowly dragged across his flesh. Neil gasped and jumped a little in her grasp.

Neil cringes in response to the loud, laughter-filled howl. They let go of him, and he watched dumbfounded as the blonde leader snorted.

"I'm not gonna eat ya! Man, when you broke in last time, I knew you were an Abeyant. I just had to wait for you to show up again!" she explained between her fits. His eyes narrowed, the shock giving way to a blaze of frustrated anger. Clenching his jaw, he got to his feet.

“What the fuck are you on about!?” he yelled at the blonde woman. “If this is some kind of sick joke, I’m out of here!” Neil turned on his heels, and two bulky-looking guys stood in his way. They crossed their arms, giving the young Neil a smug grin. Both exposed their sharp fangs.

“Sorry, but you’re not going anywhere.” Neil turned to the leader. She was more composed, taking another drag from her cigarette. “Oscar, take this kid to his new room.” A young man stepped from the crowd, looking at Neil with anxious eyes, and took a deep breath. He fidgeted with his fingers, moving and tapping them together.

“I’m not going anywhere with you,” Neil's words slid out like the hiss of a serpent, his eyes aflame with mistrust. The anxious, blonde, crazy, curly-haired vampire just stared at their blonde leader. Her gaze weighed down on Neil, crushing his resolve, while Oscar hesitated, as though contemplating his next move.

"You don't get a choice, kid," the leader snarled at Neil. Neil focused his attention back on the leader, glaring at the blonde woman.

"It's not kid. It's Neil. Bitch," he barked. The leader just smirked at him and stalked closer to him, blowing smoke into his face. Neil coughed the smoke out of his lungs.

"The name's Fallon, not bitch," Fallon snickered. "But everyone in this room has the luxury to call me that," she laughed before snapping her head over her shoulder. "Oscar, get moving."

Oscar was by Neil's side in seconds. He put his hand on Neil's shoulder, but Neil was quick to slap it off. Dragging his feet along the concrete floor, following the twitchy vampire.

Both Oscar and Neil walked down the dark hall, hindering Neil's vision.

"Ya know, Fallon isn't so bad. She's just tough, and she looks after us. She can be a real sweetheart when she wants to. Trust me, you'll like it here. We're like one enormous family. Everyone looks out for each other, and you never go hungry." Neil's ears went numb to Oscar's incessant prattle, his focus elsewhere. His hands were out in front as a barrier between him and the unknown. Oscar guiding Neil through the darkened hallways and prevent the human from bumping into walls and turning in the wrong direction.

"I forgot humans can't see, man. I've only been a vampire for five years and already forgot what's its like.

Desmond, the guy holding you down, he turned me. It's nice to know that I will not be the runt anymore or the butt of everyone's joke. Oh, that reminds me we'll need to get you human food. I wonder how long will Fallon let you be human for? Oh," Oscar grabbed Neil's shirt. Neil would let it slide for now, considering he couldn't see where he was at the moment. "This is our room," Oscar spoke again. "Sorry that you have to share, but then again, so does everybody. It saves up more space, considering how small the warehouse is and how we built a cellar, and there are so many of us." With each additional word from Oscar, Neil felt his nerves fraying, barely suppressing the urge to shout.

Neil heard the door squeak open, the hinges creak, and they pushed Neil inside. A light flickered on. Neil had to squint and blink a few times before adjusting to the brightness. It was just a simple square box, a door next to the bed on the left side of the room, a set of drawers next to Neil fit together side by side, just missing the bracket of the doorway, two beds on either side of the room, and a small window in the centre. They refurbished the floor with a horrid aqua carpet and painted the walls white. On the left wall, posters of girls in bikinis in precarious poses sticky-taped on.

Neil looked at Oscar. He could only shrug at Neil and walked to his bed, plopping himself onto the soft mattress. Oscar then pointed to the door next to his bed. “That’s, uh, the bathroom. We have a toilet in there, so yeah."

Neil only stood at the doorway, watching Oscar make himself comfortable. He looked over at Neil, giving him a nervous smile.

Please, anyone else but him!

"Don't just stand there. Make yourself at home," Neil cringed at the word.

Home? Nothing about this situation was home! Neil glared at the nervous vampire. Oscar shot up from his bed, preparing himself for the worst.

"I'm not staying," Neil's words came out as a venomous whisper, each syllable laced with defiance.

"But you can't! Fallon says you must stay!" Oscar shouted.

"And you listen to her?" Neil snarled! Oscar shrank back a little.

"W-well, s-she's our leader. She protects us!" Oscar stammered. His fingers danced in an awkward ballet, tapping against each other as if trying to find a rhythm in his anxiety. “A-and she terrifies me,” Oscar admitted.

“For a vampire, you are pathetic,” Neil deadpanned, and Oscar nodded his head.

“I-I know,” he agreed pathetically. “Everyone teases me for it, not cruelly, just that I’m new and my human quirks are still present after all this time. It will go away. Just need t-time,” Oscar rambled on, and Neil groaned.

“Stop talking!” Neil yelled at him, and Oscar shut his mouth. “I’m gonna get out of here, whether she likes it or not,” Neil explained. Oscar opened his mouth, but Neil was quick to act. “Ah! Not a word.” Oscar closed it again and nodded, shifting in his bed and laying back down.

Neil moved to his feet and approached the bed with caution. He hesitated before finally lowering himself onto the mattress. He noticed how soft but firm the bed was, feeling the warm fabric of the blanket under his skin. The last time he was in a bed, he couldn't remember. Neil looked over at Oscar. He watched the vampire close his eyes and roll over to his side. The pitch-black sky loomed over, and not a single star was in sight.

"What are you doing?" Neil asked. Oscar shifted over to face Neil, frowning before yawning at the human.

"Trying to sleep," Oscar replied.

"But it's night. Don't you burn up in the sun?" Oscar snorted out a laugh.

"No, that's just a fairytale," Oscar chuckled, his eyes threatening to close again. "Besides, you need to get some sleep too," he added and closed his eyes once more.

"I... already slept," Neil replied, looking back at the window. "I slept all day," he shrugged.

"Where?" Neil hesitated to answer. Oscar waited patiently.

"In an alley," Neil looked back at Oscar, his brow furrowing as his eyes were closed.

"And you want to go back instead of a warm bed and a place where they provide you with food?" Neil didn't respond. He just let his mind wander off. A begrudging acknowledgment tugged at the edges of his mind; Oscar's argument made an annoying amount of sense. A warm bed, food, and protection. It would be foolish to run away from it all.

Blog 30 – Part 3

Date: August 25th
Time: 2PM

The soft mattress beneath him and the vampire's stillness beside him provided Neil an unexpected sense of ease. He found it paradoxically disconcerting how comfortable he felt here compared to the open alley where he used to sleep. It was nice. It was unfamiliar to him, and it made him feel uneasy when he felt the pleasant emotion.

His stomach twisted and emitted a low growl in protest. He grimaced at the feeling, hoping the vampire next to him was still asleep. Neil could not go for another minute of his nervous chatter. Kicking the blanket off, Neil made his escape from the chattering vampire. Though he had no clear exit strategy for leaving the warehouse, he sensed deep down that he wouldn't be staying forever. Neil opened the white door, poking his head through the crack. He looked on either side of the dimly lit hallway walls.

At least I can see.

Neil wriggled through the gap between the door and the door frame, scared that he may wake the jumpy vampire. Neil poked his head back in, ensuring Oscar hadn't moved during Neil's escape. The vampire was still sprawled out on the bed, the blanket and pillow strewn across the floor. Neil stuck his head out and closed the door, hearing it lock. He waited, and nothing came from the other side. Neil could feel his own heart race, breathing a small sigh of relief, and continued to inhale the air. He hadn't realised he had been holding his breath.

Neil paused at the intersection, his eyes darting from one shadowy corridor to the next. He had Oscar guide him through the halls at night, and Neil couldn't see a darn thing. But now he could notice the vinyl flooring, painted white walls, and narrow hallways filled with many wooden doors on either side. If Neil had to take a guess, all the bedrooms were here. No matter what, Neil had to be silent. He wasn't ready to face too many vampires alone, no matter how nice they were. His social skills weren't the best.

Neil's nose decided for him. His stomach roared and echoed in the dead hallway. Neil was half expecting all the sleeping vampires to get up. Neil's fear dissipated as the delightful aroma of bacon wafted back into his nose, reminding him which direction he should take. His nose took him left, right, left again, and right once more.

Like a mouse in a one-way maze, Neil found himself irresistibly drawn to the bacon aroma wafting through the air. Neil stopped, feeling exposed as he stood on the open floor of the warehouse out of the maze-like halls.

Neil recognised the single lamp hanging from the custom-made roof but not the space he was standing in. What was once been a dark abyss was now cut-up pieces of vinyl flooring scattered along the concrete. Chairs and tables oddly placed around; some were thick cotton armchairs, old and tattered, with old bloody dried patches, and others were old hard plastic for the lawn outside. Playing cards and playing chips left on one table, dirty mugs and beer bottles left on others, ashtrays filled to the brim, just threatening to spill over and create even more mess. Neil noticed him standing underneath the large steel staircase, painted a metallic red. He remembered going up against some stairs when he first came to rob this place. Looking up, he could see the high tin roof ceiling in between the gaps.

His stomach issued another growl, as if challenging him to ignore its demands. His feet moved, coming out of the messy common space, taking one step at a time on the giant steel steps. Each step he took echoed. No matter how careful he tried to be, he sounded like an elephant stampeding through. Reaching the top, he found another shared space with more chairs and tables. Behind them were large bookcases filled with books. A TV sat in the left corner close to the stairs. To Neil's right was a small dining table and behind the table was a tiny kitchen and the source of delicious food.

The blonde leader, Fallon, hummed a happy little tune, flipping the crispy bacon over. She opened a carton of eggs and grasped one of the oval-shaped eggs.

Neil jerked forward. "I didn't like eggs."

Fallon stopped midway, close to cracking the egg against the pan. Neil's cheeks flushed, his heart rate increased. He looked away from the leader and stared at his feet.

"That's if you're cooking for me," Neil stuttered over his words. Kicking himself for how he was acting, meek, scared, and polite. He wouldn't be like this if he were out on the street.

On the streets, Neil was a different person, demanding, his eyes hard and his fists ready, ever willing to go toe-to-toe with anyone. He wouldn't care if someone was making him breakfast. Why would he assume, vampires or not, they might still enjoy consuming it? Neil's hands quivered, his whole body trembling like a leaf caught in a gust of wind. The last time he acted out like that under someone’s roof, it didn’t end well.

“No egg, got it,” Fallon’s words snapped Neil out of his torrential panic. Focusing his attention on the blonde vampire, he watched her grab a loaf of bread and smile at him. “You like toast?” she asked him. Neil gave a meek nod. “Bacon?” she clarified, and Neil nodded. “What about a tomato?” Fallon asked, flinging a tomato up in the air and catching it in her hand. Neil gave a small smile, but nodded in reply. She smiled in return and cut the tomato in half, both sides down in the pan, sliced the loaf, and put two pieces in the toaster.

Neil walked closer to the vampire, fascinated to watch her cook. Fallon plucked a few basil leaves from the pot on the windowsill and returned to the pan, flipping the tomatoes over and putting the leaves on top. The basil cooked, filling the top layer of the warehouse with a delightful fragrance.

Neil's stomach growled in defiance, and Fallon chuckled. "It's almost ready."

She dropped to the floor and opened the cupboard. She hummed again as she dug inside. Halfway in, her humming echoed within the cupboard. Neil could hear her over the sizzling bacon. She climbed out with an old ceramic plate. Artisan painted Chinese dragons on the rim, gold leaf decorating their scales, and depicted blue mountains in the centre, with a luscious waterfall spilling from them.

"Oh well, the only plate I can find," she shrugged and got up from the floor. Somewhere out there, an antique dealer is sobbing right now. She put the plate next to the pan and started piling the bacon and tomatoes on. Neil's mouth watered as he watched on, entranced by the magnificent food before him.

"You sit," she ordered Neil and pointed at the small dining table behind him. Too hungry to argue, Neil did what he was told and sat himself down. Fallon sat next to Neil, waiting for him to take a bite. Neil stared at Fallon, grasping the cold cutlery in his hands, all the while remaining eye contact with Fallon. "Well, c'mon on now, I didn't poison it. If I wanted to kill you, I would have done so last night," she huffed. Neil swallowed, nodding to himself. She had a point. It would have been his last night.

Neil enjoyed it. Little by little, he chowed down the meal prepared for him. Unable to remember the last time he had a proper meal in years.

Fallon eyed Neil's wiry frame, his clothing hanging as if it were a few sizes too large and like they could swallow him whole.

“Good to see I haven’t lost my talent for cooking,” Fallon smiled as she watched the human boy scoff the food down. “Tell me something, kid,” Fallon cut in, and Neil slowed down to look at Fallon. “How old are you?” she asked him. Neil chewed and swallowed the food in his mouth before answering.

“Sixteen,” he answered.

Fallon nodded her head. “When did you last eat?”

Neil stopped himself from taking another bite. He remained silent, and Fallon took that as an answer.

"You're that kid, who was all over the paper, the news, your parents would be worried sick," Neil dropped his cutlery. He stared down at the blonde vampire and was no longer afraid of her. He was more terrified to go back than get into a fight with a vampire.

"I'm not going back," Neil hissed.

Neil knew the truth about his home life. He ran, and they all knew that. What they didn't know about is the abuse and constant neglect he received during his entire life. He remembered the hard times, those days when he was always terrified of going back home and tried to stay longer at people's houses. People he thought he could call friends, but who all turned away when it got too much, too dangerous. No matter how much he pleaded, they always sent him back, kicking and screaming. The world turned away from him. Neil stiffened, letting the emotion in his chest rise and fall, like the ocean on a stormy night. Each memory lanced through him, as sharp as a blade.

An icy hand clasped his shoulder, snapping him out of his past. Neil took a deep, shaky breath. Wanting to flush the emotions away. Neil hoped Fallon could understand the silent screams.

"You're too young to be a vampire right now, and I don't want you to miss out on an education," she began, squeezing his shoulder for reassurance. "I'm gonna need to know what happened, and if you tell me everything, you can stay here with us. A warm bed, food, and protection until you're old enough to be one of us. Deal?" She asked Neil.

Neil stared at his lap, mulling things over. The idea sounded too good to be true. His plans for escape weren’t necessary. He didn’t want to go back to school either. The students he dealt with were dickheads. To be lured in with food, his hunger was his greatest weakness. Neil met Fallon's gaze, his eyes hardening for a moment before he nodded, sealing their unspoken pact.

“I still don’t want to go to school,” he huffed. Fallon burst out into laughter.

Blog 31 – Part 4

Date: Aug 25th
Time: 2:07PM

Neil searched his last words, baffled at how they had ignited such fury in the leader. The blazing wrath behind her eyes, the sharp dangerous fangs jutting from her lips, body tensed and ready to pounce. Neil only spoke of the truth.

Neil caught the sideways glances, the held-back whispers as he walked by. He felt the disparity between how they treated him and the other children. It surprised him that he even lasted to childhood. Only bits and pieces of his memory remain of an elderly woman smiling at him, feeding him, bathing him. Neil knows she had something to do with his upbringing, but it all changed when she disappeared. He doesn't remember who she is to him or what happened to her, but things haven't been the same since then.

Envious of the characters in his tattered books, jealous of his peers as they embrace their loved ones at the school gates. The unconditional love they have for their child, Neil yearned for that. He wanted a family to love him and he wanted it so bad.

He tried to please his parents, make them like him, but it never went as planned and in the end, Neil stopped trying. He rebelled and made things even worse. Running away was the best option he had.

Each returned kindness from his parents, now carried a shadow, a hook hidden within sugared words. The school and people he believed he could trust had also played a role in this ordeal. He wanted to escape, and the streets became his only option. Each classroom, every hallway corner at school, felt like a trap waiting to spring.

🩸🩸-----(ヽ(•̀ᵥᵥ•́)ノ)-----🩸🩸

As Neil's tale came to an end, Fallon's face tightened, her fingers curling into fists. She rose from her seat, stomped down the red staircase. Neil followed, but stopped at the top, watching Fallon open the back door and slam it behind her. The sound echoed, bouncing against the tin roof, and it seemed like all of Australia could hear it.

🩸🩸-----(ヽ(•̀ᵥᵥ•́)ノ)-----🩸🩸

Fallon had returned that night. Her hands coated in a thick layer of blood, small drops falling onto the concrete floor, her mouth drenched in red, staining her pale white skin, and her eyes blazing with the lust of the kill. Her nose flared as she approached the small human, taking in the sweet but bitter scent and bringing the leader back to consciousness.

The young boy tried to speak, but she beat him to it. The world around him became muffled. Neil's legs felt like jelly, and he collapsed to the floor, tears springing to his eyes as he stared at the cold vinyl floor.

Dead, both of them. The looming dread buried in his chest melted away, the fear leaving his lungs, and relief washed over him. He didn't have to go back. He didn't have to suffer their wrath anymore.

In a single day, he felt the deep burning rage, to the sweet release of relief. Neil reflected on his conversation with Oscar after Fallon left the warehouse in a murderous rage.

'That's why she's our leader,' Oscar's voice rang through Neil's head. *'She deals with injustices life had*

dealt us, fighting for everyone. Though I believe she seems to take the universe on her shoulders a little too much.'

Again, too much talking for Neil's liking, but it's true. His parents, no, the people meant to look after him, care for him, love him, were dead. No longer did they have a say in his life, and no longer could they torture him. He wasn't even angry at Fallon, only thankful.

That was until she forced him to go to school.

🩸🩸-----(\(•ᵥᵥ•)/)-----🩸🩸

"I hate you," he murmured to her as they both walked together toward Neil's new school. Fallon, having taken it upon herself after pulling a few strings, became Neil's legal guardian and had the final say in which school he should go to. Which, of course, entailed the most prestigious school in Melbourne.

Neil's eyes tightened every time he passed a group of well-dressed, self-important students. They received everything in life with a silver spoon. He despised those who relied on their precious money too much.

“It’s good for you,” Fallon reminded him. Neil sighed and rolled his eyes to display further disgust.

“Sure, sending me to a different hell is good for me,” he replied.

“There’s nothing wrong with learning. You’re lucky you get to go. I never had that option when I was your age,” Fallon explained. This piqued Neil’s curiosity.

“When was that?” Neil asked. Fallon stayed quiet, but smiled. Neil feared this smile as it was wicked, one full of mischief and despair. He regretted asking.

"I'll tell you about my life, little by little. Each day you go to school, you can ask me any question but only one. If you want to know more, go." Fallon smiled at Neil, fangs and all, enjoying this far too much.

"I hate you," he muttered again.

-----(＼(•ᵥᵥ•)／)-----

Neil touched his tender left cheek, wincing as he felt the throb of fresh bruises.

Neil entered the warehouse, and after learning all the ins and outs of the building, he used them to escape Oscar or a few other members who tried to be 'buddy, buddy' with him. Neil felt a strange unease around them; it wasn't dislike but a resistance to forming attachments. He had gone through that many times, only to be betrayed, and for that, he couldn't let his guard down.

Neil dropped his bag with little thought onto the floor in the middle of the warehouse and took one step.

"Pick that up," Neil jumped, feeling his skin crawl. Fallon's voice echoed within the open space of the warehouse. Neil found Fallon underneath the stairs, wearing red boxing gloves, going all out on a punching bag.

"Hey kid, how was school?" she asked him, still smashing the bag. Neil only shrugged. Not that Fallon could see it.

"Fine," he finally responded.

Fallon stopped punching the bag and turned to the young Neil, her eyes narrowing on the black and blue colours on his skin. Neil angled his face away from Fallon, letting his hair fall forward to shield his bruised eye.

Fallon took one glove off her hand and grasped Neil's chin, forcing him to look at her. Fallon's eyes widened as they landed on the black eye. Neil heard grumbling from her chest, fangs already bared.

"Who did this to you?" she hissed. Neil slapped her hand away, stepping a few feet apart. He held his silence, wrestling with the decision before him. Neil was good at handling these things himself, and the kids were never a problem. It's all of them against one, and Neil can't fight all of them. He's not some kung fu master. The boys in his school recognise him from the paper, accusing him of the murder of the people who created him. Neil refuses to call them his parents.

Fallon waited, watching his every move with a stern look. She didn't appreciate how Neil reacted, given the fact he wasn't used to social contact or this much care in his early life. It scared him a little, and he responded he only knew how.

"Sorry," Neil mumbled, looking away from her intense gaze.

"I shouldn't have acted either," she mumbled. It was barely an apology, but it's better than nothing. "You're not used to this kind of thing. I should be more patient." He agreed this was all new to him. It's scary. Neil took a deep breath, swallowing his fear, and made eye contact once more.

"It was the kids from school," Neil's voice echoed under the stairwell. Her eyes softened for a moment.

"Thank you for telling me," she whispered.

"They all hate me, and the teachers do nothing. I can't fight all of them at once," Neil swallowed afterwards.

"What do you want me to do?" she asked him.

"You could teach me how to box?"

"All right," she said, taking the gloves off and handing them over to Neil. "I can do that," she smiled. Neil grabbed the gloves, eager to slip them on. He didn't expect how difficult it is to put the second glove on.

"How do you know how to box?" he asked her.

"After I turned, I met a vampire who was very famous in the underground boxing ring, back in London in eighteen sixty-four. He taught me everything he knew," she answered.

"You're from London?" he clarified. Fallon gave the boy a sharp glare.

"Please? I just want to forget my shitty first day," he pleaded.

"Hmm, I'll indulge you in this last question," she said. "Yes, I was from London, but I've made Australia my home for the last ninety years." She answered. "Now questions are up. Let's teach you how to defend yourself," she chuffed, pushing Neil closer to the punching bag.

Blog 32 – part 5

Date: Aug 25th
Time: 2:13PM

Despite Fallon's cautionary glances and whispered warnings to the other members of the coven, Neil moved through the warehouse of vampires with an unexpected ease, as if he'd always belonged. He had started slowly taking down the walls he had built over the years. Fallon, whose steely eyes rarely softened, found herself watching Neil with something resembling warmth, a sensation foreign to her hardened demeanour.

"She's not normally this soft?"

"The boy has certainly thawed her icy heart."

"Man, she was never like that with me."

From the side glances and muttered conversations of the other vampires, Neil pieced together that Fallon wasn't the type to roll out a red carpet for an Abeyant like him. Neil could still see the shock Oscar expressed when he heard that she had been giving Neil boxing lessons.

Deep down, a question smouldered in the back of Neil's mind, fuelled by a morbid curiosity about Fallon's past. Fallon sensed something amiss when Neil stopped probing with questions and started attending school without his usual reluctance. It had taken time for Neil to build up the courage to ask everything about Fallon’s past. She froze at first. Gritting her teeth, she turned to the boy, lips pursed. Finally, she spoke.

Fallon told him that she was married off at sixteen to an old noble who had fancied her. He didn’t care how poor the family was or how small her dowry was. He wanted her all to himself. For nearly thirty years, Fallon had been living with the elderly man, hoping to find a way out.

Neil remained quiet. His features solidified into a mask of stone-like frustration. His stomach churned with the bubbling fury he felt coursing through his body. Neil couldn't imagine himself being forced to marry, even now at his age.

"No need to get so worked up," Fallon clipped him and put a chopping board in front of his face.

"But it's wrong," he muttered.

"Back then, it was normal," Fallon shrugged. Each dismissive wave from Fallon sent a fresh wave of unease rippling through Neil. "Hey!" she clapped his shoulder. He snapped out of his hardened stare and looked at Fallon like a deer in headlights. "I'm ok. I got out."

"Aye, teaching the lad how to set the place on fire?" said Desmond, a short, burly vampire with fiery orange hair.

"Yep, with you in it," Fallon retorted.

"Cheeky bitch," he laughed.

Neil grinned, quietly chuckling to himself as he overheard the conversation between the two vampires.

"How did you become in charge?" Neil asked, focusing on this one potato.

"Eh, nothing fancy. Just did what I do now, dragged Desmond's ass to Melbourne. Right, Desmond?" Desmond, too occupied with TV, grunted and waved his arm in her direction.

"So you came here and just helped others?" Neil asked.

"Pretty much. Built this little coven myself." She smiled. "Then had some long-haired vampire come in and ask if I was interested in becoming a Palatine," she growled. "It's just a fancy title for leader," she added, noting Neil's look of confusion.

"I take it you didn't like this guy?" Neil smiled, filling a pot of water.

"Nope, biggest poofter I ever saw," she snarled.

"Does this mean you have to answer to the other Palatines from the other cities?" Fallon shook her head.

"We are equals, but we answer to one vampire. He's a very special vampire, well respected throughout the world. Even opposing covens have to answer to him."

"What makes him different?"

"He's our monarchy. Clichéd as it sounds, but he rules over our asses," Fallon snorts. "Not that he's a tyrant or anything. He doesn't give a fuck about politics. All he cares about is the welfare of our species." Her smile fades, and her eyes glaze over, lost in her own memories of meeting the vampire. "We're quite fortunate to have him," she gives a sad smile.

"Fuck!" he shouts, flinching away from the stove. In a flurry, Fallon turns the stove off, rushing Neil over to the sink and running his finger under the tap.

"It's ok," Fallon soothes as she keeps Neil's finger under the tap. "It just takes practice," she breathes. Neil nods, feeling the relief of the cold water on his finger. He's scowling at himself for not moving fast enough.

"He'll kill himself before the place burns," Desmond mutters.

"Desmond!" Fallon snarls, disappearing by Neil's side, fangs already bared and holding Desmond by his shirt. The Irish vampire is shitting himself by this point, and she lectures the Irishman to keep his inner thoughts to himself and how they should stay in his head.

The burn on Neil's hand eased as he watched the lecture unfold. A small smile graced the boy's lips, and the weight in his chest lifted.

-----(＼(•̀ω•́)／)-----

High school wasn't easy for him. His peers had learned to leave him alone, ever since he beat the shit out of his bullies. Fallon's boxing lessons paid off, and his icy demeanour took care of the rest. Surrounded by a sea of humans, Neil felt like a boat adrift, unmoored and out of place. He never felt like he was one of them and preferred the company of vampires instead.

Fallon had been a constant support. Neil considered himself lucky to have graduated at all. Fallon, however, had always seen the intelligence masked by his slack demeanour. Sitting with him late at night, working with him on assignments, forcing the others to help Neil on specific topics. Desmond was good at math. Tony, another vampire who travelled from Europe to Australia, fascinated science and assisted Neil with his practical projects.

By reaching out to him in their own way, they all filled the gaping hole that had once been labelled 'family' in Neil's life.

Neil looked over at the photo in the frame on his desk, Fallon standing next to him as he held his graduation certificate. He remembered Fallon wanting to get the image processed on the same night, but the chemist was closed by the end of the ceremony.

Neil found his stride in this new, peculiar life, adapting with an ease that surprised even himself. He could only laugh at his sixteen-year-old self and the plans to run off at the first sign of escape. It took only one week for Neil to stay, go to school, and put up with his new family.

Over time, Oscar's quirks melted away, becoming less nervous, quieter, and more predator like. Neil preferred him more like this. He was less human and more like the other vampires.

Neil heard the door creak open. He stopped his pen from moving, hearing the quiet steps behind him.

“Nice try, Oscar,” Neil smiled and continued working on his uni assignment. Neil heard his friend groan but didn't stop the vampire from putting him in a headlock.

"I was so close!" Oscar cried, messing up Neil's hair. "How!?" he asked Neil.

"I heard the door and your 'loud stomping'," Neil exaggerated, and Oscar let him go. Neil watched the vampire land on his bed.

"I wasn't even stomping," Oscar defended. Neil shook his head at his brother and return to his paper. Oscar only amused himself for a short period before getting up to hassle Neil once more. "Soo, me and a few others are going hunting tonight. Wanna come?" Oscar asked. Neil snorted.

"You know that's pointless for me right now," he reminded Oscar, but the young vampire only shrugged. "Yeah, but you can drink, and as your best friend and brother, I must see you have fun. Meet a lady or a guy, let loose for a bit. You've been studying non-stop." Oscar put his hands on Neil's shoulders and shook him a little, emphasising the importance of fun.

Neil rolled his eyes, sighed, and put the pen down. "I'll consider it."

"Yes!" Oscar let go of his shoulders and fist-pumped the air.

"I'm going to tell the others," Neil watched Oscar run out of the room, the door swinging behind him.

It was a peaceful day for everyone in the warehouse. Many vampires were lounging around. Some were catching up with the world on the television, others were reading books in the back.

Neil found Fallon pacing back and forth in the kitchen. Cigarette in her mouth, the smog leaving from the end. On slow days, Fallon's pacing became frantic, her eyes darting as if expecting trouble to burst through the walls at any moment.

Few would dare to go near Fallon when she was like this. No matter how peaceful the city is, it does not settle her. Holding the belief something terrible will happen and she cannot stop it.

“Oi, Neil, ready to go?” Oscar raced up the steps.

“Where are you boys going?” Fallon asked Oscar. The vampire froze in place. His eyes widened and hunched into his shoulders like a tortoise.

“Um–well–the guys and I–with Neil–hunting,” Oscar stumbled over his words, just able to string a sentence together. More of the younger vampires approached the top, all freezing at their infuriated leader. Fallon gave a sweet smile and looked over to Neil.

“You agreed?” she asked Neil. Neil shrugged in response.

“I thought it could be fun.”

“Fun! Oh sure, and then hunters come in and kidnapped you because you’re human, tortured you to near death, and I have to save your ass because they!” she pointed to Oscar and the younger vampires behind him. “Haven’t bothered showing up to their lessons,” Fallon snarled at the last part, and a few other younger vampires–including Oscar–all cowered before her.

“Mum,” Neil says. Fallon snapped her attention to him. “I’ll be fine. I’ll be the one looking after them in the end. No one will suspect me anyway,” he assured her. Fallon took a deep breath.

“I know you’re a good fighter,” she assured herself, and then looked over at the group of youths.

"And if anything happens to him," she marched over, grabbing Oscar by the shirt. "You'll be wishing you were dead," she hissed. Oscar nodded frantically.

"We'll look after him, I swear!" Oscar whimpers.

🩸🩸-----(\(•ᵥᵥ•)/)-----🩸🩸

Neil stopped himself for a moment. He smiled at the warm memories. He seemed to be so far away, not even I could reach him.

"Nothing happened, thankfully," he chuckled softly. "Oscar wouldn't leave my side that entire night. He was so scared that something would happen to me." Neil took a deep breath, raking his finger through his hair. I could tell he was holding back. He wanted to remain neutral, unemotional, a robot, but the more he delved into his past, the more he faced the wounds he desperately tried to patch over and heal. He crumbled.

Blog 33 – part 6

Date: August
Time: 2:13PM

Neil graduated from Uni in 1984 and decided twenty-four was the right age to be a vampire. He didn't want to wait any longer. Fallon was happy to turn him earlier, but Neil wanted Uni to be over.

Those three days took a considerable toll on his body. For the last three months, his days blurred into nights of prolonged sleep and endless hunts. They considered him a baby until after six months.

After a long night's hunt, both Oscar and Neil made their way back home. Oscar slung his arm around Neil's shoulders as they returned from a hunt. Their shared laughter and unspoken understanding made it clear: they weren't just friends; they were brothers. They went out drinking, partying, and eventually hunting.

Before heading inside, Neil grabbed the bowl he left for the stray cat, checking on the second bowl to see if it had enough water.

"I don't know why you keep feeding it. Animals hate us, remember?" Oscar reminded Neil, but Neil only shrugged.

"I got to pat it a few nights ago when it was eating," Neil beamed, feeling victorious. Oscar rolled his eyes and punched his brother in the shoulder.

"Whatever," Oscar shrugged and opened the door, bowing. "After you, lovely lady," he sang. Neil laughed and curtsied. "Why, thank you, good sir."

They both walked in, laughing at themselves, but they stopped midway and found Fallon talking to an unknown vampire with noticeably long, brown, curly hair. The stranger gave a sweet smile, and Neil straightened himself, glaring back. He gave a warning growl to the vampire.

"Neil," Fallon interjected. "I would like you to meet a member of our coven," she summoned. Neil walked over to the vampire, and Oscar stayed in his place.

"I take it you're from the other worlds?" Neil asked. Fallon nodded. The stranger put his hand out.

"You must be Fallon's protégé. I'm Bellamy, Palatine of Melbourne, in the Eartharis world. It is a pleasure to meet you." Neil shook his hand. As much as he hated the slight gesture, he mustn't be rude to their guests from the other worlds.

"Neil," was all he responded, letting go of the vampire's hand. Bellamy could only shrug and continue to smile. Neil's eyes narrowed, studying Bellamy's persistently cheerful expression. A chill crept up his spine; he could sense the deception behind the smile.

"Well, I must take my leave. I shall see you at the meeting, Fallon," Bellamy dismissed himself. We all watched him exit the building, leaving the three of us alone on the main floor.

"Meeting?" Neil looked at Fallon. She sighed, rubbing her temple.

"I have asked for help. We have a problem, a werewolf problem," she explained. "And I need you to come with me," she ordered.

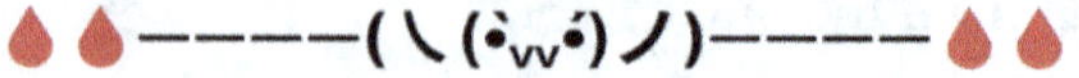

Ever since Neil had stepped into this supernatural world, the influence of the Magiqs had been a constant topic among his coven. They are the ones who created the pathways to the worlds in between. They developed a system of doors and symbols, visible only to them. However, if they are kind enough to grant you the "Magiqs Sight," you gain the ability to see these symbols, making it easier to access the doors to the other worlds.

Fallon had an old lover or friend with benefits, as she liked to call it. They always left on good terms, and she graciously gave Fallon's coven the sight, and now it was Neil's turn. Neil sat, anticipation turning into nervous energy that spilled into a rhythmic jiggle of his leg. He could hear quiet chuckles from behind him but couldn't bring himself to stop.

"Just ignore them," Fallon reassured Neil. He nodded, still jiggling his leg.

A petite woman, hinting a burning scent of marijuana, carrying a leather handbag, wearing a long dark green dress with patched flowers sewn in various shapes and colours, came up the steel staircase. She wore a flower crown upon her long golden locks, her bright blue eyes shining like the ocean on a clear sunny day. Indeed, she was stunning, but she had eyes for one person and one person only — Fallon.

"Fallon!" she shouted, running up to the vampire and jumping into her arms, embracing each other in a long kiss.

"Oh, get a room, you two!" we heard Desmond call out. They pulled away, laughing at each other.

"So you're the little son I have heard so much about," she squealed.

Little?

Neil looked over at Fallon, who just shrugged. Neil looked back at the witch, rummaging through her bag before pulling out a red vial.

"Ok, just need to put this in your eyes, and you will be set," she announced, getting on the chair next to Neil and kneeling on it. Neil was hesitant at first, but he tilted his head back and let the witch put the drops in his eyes. They stung at first, feeling like glue. The witch's warm hands grabbed his cheeks and mumbled a spell. After a few breathy seconds, she was done.

"What is this stuff made of?" he asked, his eyes shut tight.

“Oh, just a few herbs and some of my blood,” he heard her high-pitched voice answer. Neil blinked the goop away but noticed one major thing. He couldn’t see.

“Why can’t I see?” he asked, panicked, and the room erupted with laughter.

“Oh, don’t worry, it’s just a side effect. It takes your sight for a day,” she explained.

“What! No one told me this!” Neil screamed, and everyone laughed even harder. “I swear to god when I get my vision back!” he shouted again.

“Thanks, Cherry. How much do I owe you?” Neil heard Fallon.

“Don’t worry, this is the most amusing reaction I have seen. Besides, I remember you owing me a date,” Cherry answered.

"Goddamit!" Neil yelled as he knocked into the chairs, his arms flailing about.

"Oscar, help him," Neil heard Fallon yelling.

🩸🩸-----(\(•ᵥᵥ•)/)-----🩸🩸

Each claw mark and scar the coven carried bore testimony to a decade-long struggle against the same relentless werewolf pack. With each fight, it got harder to eliminate them all. Ferals were just beasts. They were easier to kill, but purebreds provided a challenge to his family.

They had lost Desmond a few months back. For weeks after the loss, Oscar became a closed-off shadow, his conversations limited to grunts. Only recently had he started sharing laughs and words with Neil again. Neil remembered Fallon's words when they first lost a member in this fight ten years ago.

“We are immortal, but we cannot escape death, and when it is time for death to take us, the ones who remain grieve, taking the loss harder than humans,” said Fallon. “We all believe we can escape death and stay in the perfect state of existence, but that is not always the case. Hunters and wolves are aware of this, leaving one member alive to deal with the loss. That is when death is desired by vampires. Their reasons to live disappear.”

“Have some vampires ever continued living after losing everything?” Neil asked his mother, looking for a shred of hope.

“There are a rare few, but it takes a lot of will to be pulled back up,” she explained. Neil's jaw tightened, his eyes darkening as he digested Fallon's words. He wanted to protect his family at all costs. He couldn’t bear the thought of losing all of them.

“Hey, don’t worry,” Fallon gripped Neil into a bear hug. “We’ll be fine, I promise,” she smiled. Neil hugged Fallon back, trying to find comfort in her assurance. Yet, a gnawing feeling in his gut whispered doubts he couldn't ignore.

🩸🩸-----(\(•ᵥᵥ•)/)-----🩸🩸

“My gut feeling was right,” Neil choked out, his voice tinged with bitterness. “They attacked our home a week later. No matter how well we fought, they outnumbered us.” His fists clenched as he finished his last word. A growl rose in his chest, fangs bared, his eyes distant, facing an imaginary opponent.

Blog 34 – Part 7

Date: Aug 25th
Time: 2:25PM

Fallon and Neil made their way home after a successful hunt. It wasn't unusual for a parent and their child to hunt together, building a stronger relationship. Walking through the empty streets, they laughed and boasted about who was the better boxer or who was the fastest runner. Neil grinned, his steps light, as if each jab they threw at each other was another form of upliftment.

Their laughter died down, and the city's silence welcomed them. Cars passed them by, and they heard distant shouts from one apartment inside, drunken scrawlers, no doubt. It had gotten busier over the years. Fallon remembered how desolate the nights were in the early hours of the morning. So much had changed since she first arrived in Australia. Fallon enjoyed the peace from time to time. She hooked her arm over Neil’s shoulder and gave a light squeeze.

“You know I’m proud of you,” she murmured. “You’ve come a long way since we first met, and I couldn’t be prouder,” she smiled at him. Neil's chest expanded noticeably, and his lips tightened as if to keep a secret smile from escaping. He could feel his eyes water and diverted his gaze so as not to appear weak. It was so unexpected. He was used to her praise, but this was out of the blue.

“Neil,” Fallon became concerned from his lack of eye contact.

“I’m okay,” he laughed, wiping the stray tear from his eye.

"For a second, I thought you were crying," she teased.

"Me? Never!" he retorted, though she snorted at the younger vampire and ruffled his hair. Neil batted her hand away with a wide grin.

"There is one more thing, something I have been meaning to ask you–well, more like tell you and hope you take it on," Fallon rambled. Neil raised his brow, his pace slowing a little.

"What is it?" he asked her with urgency.

"Nothing serious," she assured him, but with pursed lips and narrowed eyes, he didn't believe her. "If, and I'm just saying if, not like it will happen, but I want you to take over, look after the city, the coven, all of it," Fallon proposed. Neil's posture eased; his tense shoulders fell, but his eyes remained fixed in a scowl

"Where will you be?" he asked.

"In Hawaii, hopefully, taking a break," she chuckled. Neil breathed a sigh of relief, but Fallon stopped them both as she left her hand on his shoulder. "But I may not be around either. With these mutts, anything can happen," Fallon urged. "I just want you to know that I'm always proud, and I know you will make an outstanding Palatine," she pulled Neil into a tight grip hug. Neil held onto her tight, afraid to let his mother go.

Neil sniffled a little as he let go. He caught the distinct smell of smoke and looked in the direction they were heading. Black, thick smoke rose into the murky sky. Fallon and Neil both hurried back home, hoping to some higher power that it wasn't their house.

The warehouse burned in a fiery blaze, and a pack of werewolves stood before the burning building. One half waited for survivors escaping the inferno as bodies lay strewn on the ground, unbeknownst to the waiting danger outside as they escaped. The other half of the pack fought back against Neil's coven. In their human form, werewolves were vulnerable like humans, but they made up for this with their abilities when they transformed into beasts.

Neil recognised the vampire in one of their grasps. Oscar thrashed about, snarling insults at all of them, kicking and screaming for them to let him go. Neil's eyes narrowed, his canines peeking out over his lower lip as his fingers grew into claws. The werewolves outnumbered them, and he knew that, but he couldn't leave his brother behind. He had to save him. He had to save someone he cared about.

The rest of the pack shifted into their forms, charging at the two vampires. Fallon was quicker to react, weaving through the pack, using her sharpened claws to slice into their soft flesh, aiming for the jugulars as she cut through them. A burly wolf struck Neil down, fighting back against the giant beast on top of him. One werewolf was easy enough to handle, but an entire pack was another story. He kicked the giant wolf off and snapped its neck, but another wolf tackled Neil to the ground once more. Each growl Neil let out became more pronounced, more irritated. He wanted this fight to be over, and he wanted it done now. Neil ripped the heart out from the other, its snapping jaws missing his face. He was lucky to be alive.

Neil charged for Oscar, with Fallon by his side, dodging and slicing at the dogs coming for them as they charged. There was still time to save him.

The leader, growing impatient with his pack's idiocy and lack of teamwork, took matters into his own hands. His right hand changed into sharp, black claws, and he grew thick, brown fur from his elbow down to his arm, becoming muscular. The head of the pack stalked over to Oscar, a wicked grin forming on his face as he did. The wolf grunt holding Oscar presented the young vampire to their leader with a wolfish grin.

"No!" Neil pushed himself to run faster, throwing any werewolf that dared to tackle him to the ground. In these moments, the world around you appeared to stand still and become crystal clear. Even though you may feel you're moving quickly, the universe can still be cruel with every step leading up to this moment.

With a last thrust, the leader tore into Oscar's chest. Neil faltered, falling to his knees. Blood spilled from Oscar's mouth, his hands ripping at the fur of the mutt holding his heart captive. The dog paid no mind as clumps of fur ripped from his skin. Oscar kicked and snarled, desperation screaming from his eyes. With a smile, the leader ripped his heart out of his chest. Oscar's body went limp in his captor's arms. Neil could only watch in horror.

Neil clutched his chest as though physically trying to hold it together, his face contorted in an expression of indescribable agony. They had lost so much. Everyone in his life was dropping one by one.

"Neil!" Fallon screamed his name.

A wolf knocked Neil off his feet. His skin scraped against the hard concrete, snapping him back into reality. He struggled to his feet and fell back onto his knees. He hissed from the sharp pain, watching his palms heal. Neil looked up, searching around the carnage before him. His voice caught in his throat, his body frozen in place, and his heart breaking all over again. This moment was ten times worse than watching Oscar die before his eyes.

'No, no, please no.'

Blood flowed like a waterfall through her chest and the muscular dog's arm tore into the back of her spine, destroying her rib cage. Its enormous claws just miss her heart. Fallon was holding on. She glanced at Neil with a weak smile.

"No," he whispered.

"Love–you." The werewolf widened its massive jaws, tearing Fallon's head off just as she finished her last words.

Neil just sat, his eyes wide and unfocused, as if the flames rising around him were freezing him into a still life. His loved ones, the home he had built, all burning to ashes.

Neil looked at the snarling pack, then slowly closed his eyes. What he held dear was now gone. He could only hope these dogs had a shred of decency and finish him. Neil crumbled to the ground, weeping.

Gone–all of it–everyone–no–please–don't leave me.

A pair of leather shoes came into view. Neil looked up, face to face with the grinning leader of the pack. Like the madman he was, he just laughed at Neil and clicked his fingers. The pack descended on Neil. Tearing into flesh, Neil didn't scream. He didn't beg or cry. He was numb.

"Make sure he survives, boys. Death for this one is mercy."

🩸🩸-----(＼(•ᵥᵥ•)ノ)-----🩸🩸

I took a shaky breath myself. A weary light dancing behind Niel's eyes, as if he were a candle burning at both ends. His hands trembled, clenching and unclenching as if trying to grasp onto fragments of a life he'd been patching together for decades with nothing more than tape and glue.

"Nathaniel and Brooklyn found me a day later." His voice cracked, but he cleared his throat before continuing. "I hated them at first, hated that they saved me, forced me to live. I never–tried–I just waited instead, hoping I would draw enough attention to myself. Maybe a hunter would come and kill me, a werewolf, or they'd push me away." Neil swallowed. The afternoon light hidden on the horizon, greeted by the early evening sky. "With Brooklyn's persistent–'nagging'–Nathaniel's impressive–'speeches'." Neil added.

We both snorted, understanding how persistent Nathaniel was. He could give legendary speeches of encouragement and valour. It could lift anyone's morale up. He delivered them to Brooklyn a pretty fair bit–well, when he wanted to get his own way–Nathaniel should have been a politician, not gonna lie. "They grew on me," he whispered. "I stayed, I tolerated life."

It was a rare moment to see Neil this vulnerable, baring his soul. It made sense, all of it.

"I don't want to get close. I don't want my past to repeat itself." Tears welled up in Neil's eyes, bursting through the barrier and trickling down his cheeks. "I don't want to go through it all over again. If I allow myself a moment of happiness, they will take it away from me again," Neil sniffled, shaking like a leaf in a tornado. "Damnit," he hissed, rubbing his eyes. "How do you do this to me?" he snarled.

The sweet, vulnerable Neil cowered back into his hardened shell. "I never told Brooklyn or Nathaniel, and yet I am spilling my guts to you. Do you know how frustrating that is?" he snarled, baring his fangs at me. "No matter how hard I try, you always could break me." Remaining silent, watching the vampire cry for what I presume is the first time in decades.

Grabbing my laptop, I stood up from the table and maintained eye contact with the sniffling vampire.

"I don't know what sparked it. I don't know why I am the cause, but I can say a deal is a deal." I told him. Neil watched me with watery eyes, tears streaming down his cheeks. "You opened up just so you can get rid of me, ensuring your sullen existence remains intact. I know you want to be happy again, but your fear consumes you to the point you would get rid of it yourself." I gave Neil a sad smile and leaned forward, my lips touching his cold forehead. "Thanks for letting me stay for a while," I murmured, pulling away and walking back inside.

Blog 35

Date: Dec 4th
Time: 9AM

'I have been gone for a while and I never expected to receive so many messages or prayers for my wellbeing. My sincere apologies to my devoted readers. I am sorry for not being around. I didn't mean to disappear from you all for the last three months. These posts will explain my absence, clearing the air why I have disappeared for so long.

But in the end I can't keep this blog going for much longer. I will keep this up for anyone who stumbles upon it, but I will have to change names once I have finished writing it. Forgive me.'

I grabbed the last pieces of clothing, packing them in a duffle bag. I slid the hunting knife Brooklyn gave me into the back of my pants. I double-checked the hunting knife's position, feeling its reassuring weight. Shadows loomed in the alleyways as I thought of the lurking dangers.

Atem seemed keen on guiding my every step, weaving in and out between my legs as I walked. The mischievous feline made himself at home in my luggage, leaving his mark with a purr and a generous shedding of his golden fur onto my black clothes.

I wanted to bring one dress Nathaniel gave me, but it would take up half of my bag. With a heavy heart, I forced myself to close the door and never look back. The photo of my dad made me wonder what he would say to all of this? Vampires? Are you on drugs? No, dad.

I laughed at my internal monologue and put the photo inside the bag. A subtle vibration against my thigh caught my attention.

'So, I was thinking about lots of pizzas and a movie tonight. You in?' Brooklyn.

Thanks to my help, he had learned the way of the millennia. I was also the one to thank for Brooklyn's particular taste for human food, much to Nathaniel's disgust, reminding Brooklyn that it did nothing for him. I wanted to reply. My thumb hovered over the keyboard, tempted by the thought of pizza and an endless playlist of movies.

I slid open the phone, giggling at the silly face Brooklyn chose for his chosen profile pic. Scrolling through our conversations, I remembered him discovering the camera and me explaining selfies to him.

He sent me the worse faces possible. Now he liked to keep me updated with his garden when I'm at work. His earlier photos were of the couch, his beard, and his foot at one point.

Nathaniel was still stubborn and hopeless to manage his own before finally giving in and accepting help. Both Brooklyn and Nathaniel were learning from each other. Two happy dummies.

With a sad smile, I replied, lying that I had a shift on tonight.

Atem kept lying on my duffle bag, relentless in his pursuit to put fur all over my clothes. Every time I removed him, I turned away and back, just to find him in the same spot. Atem was insistent on hindering my packing. He knew something was up. In a final push, he brushed up against my legs, trilling to get my attention.

Those beautiful blue eyes stared into mine. I gave his head one more gentle pat, his fur soft against my skin. I was going to miss him.

Zipping the duffle bag, I looked back to the writer's desk Nathaniel had given me. I smiled at the large wooden desk adorned with pop vinyls and plush toys.

Nathaniel always complained about the nick-nacks; he'd probably welcome its absence.

Brooklyn would give my peace lilies the love they deserved.

Atem rubbed against my legs again, meowing. I smiled at the little kitty, picking him up, patting him. I rocked back and forth like any mother would do for their baby. As I cradled him in my arms, he purred and looked at me with his sleepy eyes. The sudden knocking at my door brought our special moment to an abrupt end. Neil opened the old oak door. Giving a weak smile, he nodded.

I took a deep breath in and kissed Atem on the forehead, and placed him on the hardwood floor below. Retrieving my bag and pulling it over my shoulder, I shuffled over to Neil and gave a small smile of my own.

"Look after Atem for me, OK?" Neil nodded his head. We both looked down at the said cat, who was rubbing against both our legs. "Same goes for you, Atem," I whispered, patting his head one last time.

I walked out of my old bedroom, making my way to the living room, reminiscing one last time. The bickering between Nathaniel and me, the long talks in the garden with Brooklyn, the freak summer storms, Brooklyn and Nathaniel having a screaming match about the wet trail Brooklyn left behind. Whenever I made a meal, Nathaniel had a look of absolute disgust, no matter how good it looked. Brooklyn's advice for life situations, Nathaniel's feedback to improve my writing, and the never-ending cups of tea when I was around Nathaniel. I wouldn't miss the constant questions from Brooklyn regarding our slang and the endless bickering between all of them.

Looking back, it was hard to believe how far we'd all come—these lovable, infuriating idiots had become my family.

This was home. This was my family, as much as I hated leaving it. Laughter, arguments, shared silences. These moments made this place special. With one last sigh, I made my way to the large oak door. I turned back to Atem and Neil with a last smile. I opened the door, saying goodbye one last time.

Blog 36

Date: Dec 4th
Time : 9:05AM

'For this part of the post, I'm going to write about what happened after I left. Brooklyn and Nathaniel filled me in on this. So please cue rage.'

It was late since Brooklyn and Nathaniel had returned home. Brooklyn and Nathaniel trudged in, their shoulders slumped, carrying the weight of the seven tedious days Bellamy had put them through. Brooklyn was prepared to toss Nathaniel into the river for suggesting he was the one to do the more hazardous jobs. Brooklyn's piercing stare sent shivers down Nathaniel's spine as they walked in.

Nathaniel eyed the spiral staircase leading to his secluded tower, a sanctuary with books and tea, weighing whether he had the stamina to climb and escape Brooklyn's brewing storm.

Nathaniel gave a lazy sigh and headed for the kettle.

“Valeria!” he called, but there was no answer.

“She said something about work earlier,” Brooklyn murmured, sitting on the leather couch glued to the phone. Nathaniel caught sight of Brooklyn, face buried in the smartphone, and his eyes did an involuntary roll. To him, the device seemed to reduce centuries of human achievement to mere pixels.

“When will she be back?” he asks Brooklyn as he grabs his new favourite ‘Tea makes me happy, you not so much' mug, a gift from Valeria that nailed his personality.

"Uh–she didn't say." Brooklyn looked back to his curled, moustached friend, scratching his beard with a scowl on his face.

Neil eased his bedroom door open and stared at his two vampiric roommates with wide eyes. They noticed how tense and careful his movements were as he approached them from his room. He was never petrified unless he knew how much he fucked up and considering they had lived with him for so long. They both knew he had fucked up and bad.

"What did you do?" Brooklyn growled, jumping to his feet and slams Neil into the wall so hard that the plasterboard cracked, leaving a huge, jagged indent. Brooklyn's fangs gleamed menacingly, extending as if they had a life of their own, an inch from Neil's vulnerable neck. His blood would do nothing for Brooklyn. This was just to hurt Neil.

“She isn’t coming back,” Neil whispered, a little shaky in response. Brooklyn snarled and threw Neil back into the wall.

“What–did–you–do?” Brooklyn was at his breaking point. His tolerance for Neil had been dwindling for a while, forgiving him often, considering his wishes. Neil held Nathaniel and Brooklyn to different standards with their wishes. He never gave them the same respect, and Brooklyn had had enough.

Neil averted his eyes, as if Brooklyn’s gaze were a laser beam scorching through to his very core

“She left.” The words left Neil's lips like molten lava, searing their way out and leaving an aching void in his chest. It hurt Neil more than Brooklyn. The gaping hole in his heart grew once again. What was still and left to rot and fester for years, never healing, was now aching. He couldn't numb the pain this time.

"Left, left? What do you mean, left?!" Brooklyn screamed in Neil's ear.

"We made a deal. She's just holding up the end of her bargain." Brooklyn was shaking with rage by this point. Neil waited for the screams. He waited for Brooklyn to throw a fist at him and beat him to a bloody pulp, but no, Brooklyn did something unexpected. He let Neil go, stalked over to the leather couch, grabbed his phone, and nodded to Nathaniel. Nathaniel nodded back, understanding the silent conversation with his friend.

"By the time we come home with Valeria, I want you out," Brooklyn said, still shaking with rage. Neil knew he meant it. Neil knew he fucked up. It felt as if someone had swept his carefully assembled life puzzle off the table, scattering its pieces into the space. This is what he wants, right? He wants to be alone, secluded, cut off? Unfeeling, unemotional, so he may never have to experience the pain he went through again? This shouldn't bother him. This shouldn't be an issue. Neil should be fine leaving them both–but he isn't. Neil broke the promise he made himself from the very beginning. Don't get attached.

"I'll go to the restaurant. You see if she went to the closest station," Brooklyn began a plan of action, watching Nathaniel pour his tea into a keep cup. Music played in the quiet apartment. Neil recognised the music. It's that annoying pop-punk band that she adores. He couldn't remember the name, but he knew it related to something about pancakes. Stacks, stackers, shorts? He couldn't remember. But he knew it's her calling. Brooklyn took his phone out of his pocket, answering it with a barrage of questions. He stopped, he growled, fangs bared.

"Let her go."

Blog 37

Date: Dec 4th
Time: 9:05AM

'I know I am making these shorter, but it's easier to break up what happened in individual chapters. In this part, I am going to write off what happens to me now.'

I stood in the centre of the train station, watching the screen flash the rostered times and locations. I tried to remember which train took me to the shopping centre with the old heritage tower. It used to make lead shot bullets. It's interesting how they built a shopping centre around it. Better than destroying it.

I looked around, trying to find a safe place to stand. My eyes darted around the station as I moved further from the train roster, every glance from a passerby making me feel like I was deciphering hieroglyphs on the train schedule. They could write it in another language. That's how much trouble I am having. I found an empty corner near the entrance of a store, out of everyone's way, and looked at my phone, hoping the internet would provide the answers I needed. I remembered an old place I could rent for cheap and still be able to keep my job.

"Valeria?" I frowned, hearing the voice calling my name. I didn't recognise this voice.

I looked up from my phone and saw a familiar gentleman, styled blonde hair slicked back with too much product. White dress pants and a buttoned-up shirt, too formal for a standard setting but underdressed for a wedding. The gentleman's smile only grew. His hand morphed and shifted, large talons and fur growing, his arm becoming more muscular.

His eyes flashed yellow for a second and returned to a typical green.

“Cedric, I presume,” I swallowed.

“You remember me, so sweet!” he sang. “And here I thought I was just another mutt to you,” he chuckled, his arm shifting back to normal.

“What do you want?” I hissed.

“Cutting to the chase, very well. I am not into charades like you vampires,” he huffed, clicking his fingers.

Two other bulky werewolves came up beside me. Both of their hands morphed, their sharp talons ready to slice into me if I made any sudden movements. “I want you to come with me and tell me what your little friends are planning," he grinned.

"I do not know what you're talking about," Keeping my face unreadable, I met Cedric's eyes without a hint of emotion. Cedric threw his head back and laughed.

"Oh, I think you do," he chuckled and grabbed his phone out of his pocket. "Let's see," he hummed, reading over the text. "Here we are: 'The meeting began after–I won't bore anyone with the details, but the universe is more vast than I thought.' Sound familiar?" For a moment, I felt as if someone had hit the 'pause' button on me, freezing me in place. Hearing him mimic the inner workings of my mind as I wrote it out on the screen. Those are my words, my writing, my blog. This tickled Cedric pink. "I love what you have written and the love you have for those boys, but I am flattered you put me in your insignificant life. I was feeling left out."

Speechless, I didn't expect my blog to land me in trouble. I had thought it was harmless, a simple blog to share my inner thoughts and experiences, but they had found it, read it, and I was at a loss for words.

Cedric leaned closer to my face, our noses almost touching at this point. "Didn't anyone ever tell you–that you should never put your personal details on the internet?" Cedric snickered, pulling away and nodding to his comrades.

"Let's go," he commanded. His lackeys pushed me forward, and I moved with them, looking around my surroundings. Everyone didn't seem to notice the suspicion of three guys escorting a young woman out of the station.

They want to be normal, huh? Let's give 'em hell.

As soon as I was outside on the street, I made my move. Throwing my duffle bag at one guard and dodging the other, I made a run for it and pushed people out of the way, running as fast as I could. A jolt of raw energy shot through me, and my legs propelled me faster than I'd ever thought possible. Humans outnumber werewolves if they had to decide whether they cared to cause mayhem just by shifting and letting the world know werewolves exist or keep the secret. It's their choice.

People watched in a confused daze, not knowing if they should step in and help or worry about their safety.

The internal mantra pounded in my head like a drumbeat, driving me away from the dark, empty mouths of alleyways and toward streets, humming with activity.

I turned the corner, and my heart leapt out of my chest. One guard came into view. I turned back and saw the other prowling towards me.

The only way out is the alleyway, through to oncoming traffic. I won't make the other side. A sinking feeling settled in my stomach as I glanced between the two closing guards.

"Not bad," I heard Cedric's voice behind me. "You got the balls to run." Cedric dropped my bag onto the ground. "But I'm afraid that's just going to get you killed." He smirked.

The sharp blow to my head was excruciating; my legs gave out, and suddenly I was in darkness.

"You think people would make a fuss about this sort of thing happening right before them? Try to do something. I guess I'll never know what's going through people's heads."

Waking up felt like being yanked out of murky water; every pulse in my head was a hammer, each wince a testament to the pain. My neck felt stiff and protested with every sudden movement. As I tried to move my arms, I realised they were bound tightly with rope, restricting my freedom.

It was dark, and I couldn't see anything other than the moon's light shining from an open window.

How typical. I gave this hotel a zero-point one-star rating.

"Good to see you awake," Cedric's voice lingered in the darkness. "Comfy?" I heard him chuckle.

“Could have used a pillow,” I murmured. Cedric’s laugh lingered in the darkness.

“Oh, don’t worry, I plan to make your stay very special.” A dark heat surged up within me, a fierce glare directed at where I thought Cedric's voice emanated from. I won’t let him get away with this!

Blog 38

Date: Dec 4th
Time: 9:08 AM

It was late, my phone was gone, and they tied me to a chair. *Could my day get any worse?*

I stared up at the tin roof, the distinct salt in the air reminding me of the island I used to visit with my family. *They were happier times*.

As the darkness deepened, my eyes adjusted more easily.

The metal walls rusted away from the salty air. Old drums lay askew around the cracked concrete floor, and chains dangled around the beams of the warehouse, swaying gently in the light ocean breeze, clattering and creaking, filling the empty void of the warehouse.

'Bunch of bad guys and a warehouse. What's with bad guys and warehouses?'

I tug at the ropes wrapped around my arms once more. As I rocked my seat a few centimetres along the floor. I could feel the knife tucked into the back of my pants pressed into my back. At least they hadn't found it, but I had no chance of using it!

I gain momentum, I continued clacking and creaking. I tried to stay vigilant in case the werewolves emerged from the shadows. Each second that ticked by without the werewolves appearing felt like borrowed time.

Eventually, I managed to stand on my two feet, my rear end in the air, my legs only able to part themselves into a shuffle, and the weight of the chair held me down like a wooden shell.

'I now know what a tortoise feels like,'

I searched for broken glass or metal and spot an old rusted barrel. Its sharp rusted edges looking perfect for cutting any piece of rope. Leaning to the left, balancing the heavy chair on my back, I tried to reach the sharp barrel. However, my attempt failed, and the barrel fell to the ground with a reverberating clang before rolling into the dark abyss. I let out a frustrated groan.

"Give me a break!" I yelled into the darkness.

"Karma is a bitch, isn't it?" Cedric's voice chuckled from the shadows. I shuffled around, trying to find the werewolf.

'I could use vampire vision right now.'

I felt a pair of muscular arms grabbed me and forced me to sit back down on the chair. The chair hit the floor with a loud clack, and my butt hit the wood. I gritted my teeth, holding back the sharp pain shooting up my spine. I looked up and glared at the werewolves.

"I would tempt karma if these ropes weren't in the way," I hissed.

"Then please, let me," Cedric stepped out of the shadows, holding a knife, and took his time approaching me. With a broad smile, he cut the rope, freeing me from the chair. I got up to my feet, but his lackeys were quick to sit me down. "Sorry, but you're not going anywhere," Cedric giggled. "We have some distinguished guests, and I want you to be here."

My mind went blank, and my heart thumped in my chest as an icy fear crept over me, paralysing my muscles..

He couldn't mean...

"If you hurt them, I swear to god," I hissed as I tried to stand from the chair, only to be restrained.

"Oh, we are going to do more than that," he gloated. I clenched my jaw together as rage bubbled over.

"And what were you planning to do?" I recognised the British voice anywhere. My heart stopped another second as three figures approached from the shadows.

Brooklyn's fangs and claws were sharp, bared, ready for the battle. Rage seethed through him, and it filled the empty warehouse.

Neil was sombre as usual, but something lurked beneath his cold eyes, something resembling emotion burning away deep inside. Fear.

Nathaniel remained composed. Compared to the other two, he stood tall before the werewolves, even approaching them.

"Nathaniel, I take it?" Cedric asked. "I recognise the 'stache your little human has been writing about," Cedric chuckled and turned back to me with a wink.

"What is he talking about?" Neil snapped, his eyes boring into mine.

"Oh, that's right, you don't know." Cedric waltzed over to me, putting his rough hands on my shoulders. "You know she's been writing this cute little blog about her life and the crazy vampire roommates. It's adorable. You should read it sometime."

"Surely You didn't write a blog?" Nathaniel asked, sounding disappointed. At this moment, I felt like a child getting in trouble with the teacher for cheating on a math test. I looked away from their judgmental gaze and stared at my feet.

"I didn't expect it to get us in so much trouble, I just–I just needed to tell someone, I–fuck. I'm sorry." My voice faltered to a whisper, my throat tightening and clogs and my heart breaking in two. Guilt gnawed at my insides; my stupid blog had led us into this trap.

"It doesn't matter," Neil's voice broke the silence. "Whether she wrote the blog, you would have held her captive anyway," I heard Cedric giggle.

"You are correct. But it makes things a little easier," Cedric said with a touch of humour. "She's one of you. I can't let you all survive," he hissed.

"We can't take you all on by ourselves," Nathaniel stepped into the conversation. "But we can make a deal."

"Oh, a barter? You must care about her," Cedric teased, forcing my head up and making me look at the three vampires.

"Of course we do," Nathaniel growled, his canines bared.

"She's our family," Brooklyn finished the sentence, standing beside Nathaniel. Neil stayed behind them and watch a war battle within himself.

Cedric's laughter echoed in the warehouse.

"Oh, that's cute, but I'm not interested in making a deal anyway," Cedric grabbed the hair at the back of my head, and I bit back the yelp. He threw me to the ground, and my face was just at Nathaniel's beautiful leather shoes and Brooklyn's... thongs. Brooklyn wore thongs to the battlefield.

“I just needed bait, so I can kill you all,” Cedric finished, He snapped his fingers, and the pack descended upon us all.

I am stunned watching three vampires face off against a pack of werewolves and their leader hiding behind his underlings. They all circle, snapped their teeth and growled at the two lanky vampires and burly Brooklyn.

Their bravery baffled me; I couldn't fathom what compelled them to risk their lives for mine.

One mutt launched himself at Neil. He moved quickly, claws growing from his fingertips, fangs bared. Neil let out a feral scream, slicing the attacking werewolf in the abdomen. Blood pooled from the creature’s wound. Brooklyn showed off his impressive strength, holding one beast back with his bare hands. Nathaniel lifted me to my feet and pushed me away just in time as the wolf pounced on top of him.

"Valeria, get out of here, now!" Nathaniel screamed, struggling against the wolf, its teeth missing Nathaniel's head.

I couldn't move, my eyes glued to the chaos erupting before me. I wanted to fight back.

Three wolves lay dead at Brooklyn's feet, and he pulled the fourth from his blood-soaked arm. With a quick, brutal twist of his hand, Neil silenced another werewolf permanently. Its body morphed back to its human form. A deep, mournful howl filled the tin building, and the reverberations felt like a shockwave against my skin. The sheer number of ferocious beasts overwhelmed the boys. They threw Brooklyn and me across the warehouse, and when we landed on the concrete, I felt the impact shake through my body.

I gasped for air as I felt the wind leave my lungs. Neil lay on the ground unconscious, and Brooklyn got back into the fight. Nathaniel was successful in taking a dog on alone but suffered severe injuries. Nathaniel limped over to Neil, shaking him awake. They hurled Brooklyn backwards, cradling his side, growling ferociously at the pack and striving to stand upright. Neil jolted awake. His eyes widened, his breathing erratic, as if suffocated by his own fear. The pack circled.

"Hmm, I think I remember you," Cedric taunted as he stalked closer. "My father mentioned slaughtering an entire coven of vampires in the early eighties. Left only one alive," he continued to smile.

A memory of brief happiness flashed behind Neil's head. Neil snarled, baring his fangs, getting up to his feet, and charging at the leader head-on. Cedric was too quick. Catching Neil by the throat, he struggled to get out of the dog's transformed hand.

"Fuck you," Neil gasped. Cedric only smiled and threw Neil back, crashing into Brooklyn and Nathaniel.

"Time to die," Cedric said in a sing-song voice.

'No. I get to my feet. They can't.'

I bolted toward them, each heartbeat a drum in my ears, a rush of adrenaline driving me forward. They lay there on the ground, struggling to get back up. Cedric drew closer to them. A wicked smile grew with each step. His teeth seemed to sharpen, the excitement for the kill was upon him.

Neil looked up, his eyes widening, watching me run to the battlefield. "Don't–Valeria–stop."

I ignored his weak protests and stood before the werewolf pack, my arms stretched out, trying to shield the boys as much as possible. Cedric and his pack stopped. Laughter erupted within the space of the warehouse, echoing. Taunting me as I stood tall before them.

"And what are you going to do?" Cedric mocked. "You're just a little human. How can you stop us?" he growled, teeth sharp and bare.

"I will not let you hurt my family," I hissed. Feeling a strange sensation erupt in my chest. A piece that had been missing for so long, a part that I didn't know I needed till now. It was like a tidal wave washing over me, the urge to protect them, like a beast ready to break out with such ferocity. I was prepared to kill anything that hurt them. They all laughed at me again. Cedric practically could not control himself. He was laughing so hard, he was doubling over.

"Your family?" he continued to laugh. "You're joking, right? They'll kill you as soon as they have the chance."

"You're wrong." I took a step forward, letting my arms fall to their sides. Cedric walked up to my face, our noses touching. I moved an inch, my eyes locking with his. I didn't flinch as we stared at each other.

"Someone once told me a vampire's loyalty is the best kind of loyalty." Cedric tsked and stepped back, his wolfish smile returning once more. "And what makes you different?" he asked me. I broke away from his eyes, noticing his hand transform. Sharp talons and fur grew, his muscles morphed and became bulky. Cedric, too cocky to notice my hand snaking its way to the back of my pants. Grasping the ivory handle, clenching it in my fist. “Well–go on–what makes you different?” he taunted me further, his face near mine once more. In arm’s reach.

I smiled at the werewolf.

“Fuck you, that’s how.”

I swung my arm forward; the knife stuck into Cedric’s throat. Blood sprayed from the artery, coating my hand, the blade, his body, and the floor beneath him. With the little strength he had, I was too slow from his transformed hand. I felt the claws tear into my stomach, organs pulled from the gut, blood pooling like a flowing waterfall. I took a step back, and then I stumbled. My legs gave way.

“Fuck!” I heard Neil cry out. I landed in his stiff arms, saving me from the harsh concrete. “You idiot, do you have any idea?” he cut himself off, biting his tongue. His body trembled, eyes widening, as if he'd just heard his own death sentence.

Cedric’s pack howled, echoing throughout. I was sure all of Melbourne could hear them.

“Oh, shut up,” I recognised the voice.

Bellamy and a bunch of other vampires came in, surrounding the pack. He looked at Neil and me, giving a small smile. “Got your message, couldn’t wait–could you?” he chuckled. “Well, it doesn’t matter. We’re here now.” Bellamy winked at both of us. “Get her out here.” Bellamy pointed to the exit. “All right, everyone, let’s kill these mutts.”

Neil snapped out of his daze, picking me up and running from the battlefield.

I took a deep breath, feeling my lungs struggle to keep the oxygen in. losing the strength to keep my eyes open.

"Hey, hey, come on, stay awake, you're going to be okay," Neil propped my head with his arm, holding me close to his body. "You should have–you–goddamn it!" he screamed. "Why did you do that? You should have just run? Fuck!" Moisture gathered in the corners of Neil's eyes, threatening to spill over. The emotions inside him were like a deadly cocktail, a mix of anger, sadness, and frustration all blending together. "I could have lost you," he sobbed. "I can't lose anyone else, not to them, not again. Not when I -." He choked. "I love Nathaniel, I love Brooklyn–they're my brothers, they took me in, and I could have lost them, I could have lost them–and I could have lost you. Fuck, I love you–I love who you are. I love your quirks, your inability to socialise. Fuck, I love everything about you. You were so brave to stand against them," Neil cried.

The armour we had been chipping away for months–years, broke. All the emotions Neil had kept inside poured from him like Niagara Falls. I reached up and touched his cheek, wiping away the tear. His body no longer felt cold to me.

"Took ya long enough," I smiled. Neil half-laughed and half-sobbed. He needed us. He always did.

"I'm sorry, god. I'm so sorry!" he pressed his forehead against mine as he let out a wail of sorrow, his body trembling in despair. Neil swallowed, sucking in the air, and nodded. “It’s going to hurt, but it’s the only way,” he whispered in my ear.

Neil bit into his wrist, taking long draws from his wound. He held the blood in his mouth and then our lips locked together in an icy embrace. I felt the warmth of his blood as it flowed into my mouth, filling it with a metallic taste. The thick liquid travelled down my throat, leaving a burning sensation in its wake. It was as if tiny needles were piercing my skin and sewing it back together again.

‘Through the eyes of another person, they could have seen this as romantic. For me? It needed to be less bloody–but oh well.’

Darkness consumed me, the world became muffled, and the last thing I saw was Neil's bloody mouth moving.

Blog 39

Date: Dec 4th
Time: 9:10AM

'Um, surprise? It's a lot to take in. I'm still adjusting to the whole thing myself. It's weird not being able to eat anymore. And I sleep all the time. It sucks. All I do is eat and then sleep. I'm told it only lasts for six months and I feel like more myself each day. Three days of transformation exhaust the mind and body, it a shock to the system for such drastic changes to happen in a short period. Afterward, you rest more and after three months, you understand how to contain your hunger through discipline. Your adult mind is like a child's mind. You become shyer around other vampires, and you hide behind your sire and look for their protection during that time. It's weird. I would feel like myself, but then I don't.

Oh well, that's enough rambling on my end. I'll get back the story.'

A searing pain pulsed through my veins, flickering erratically throughout my nerves like a broken electrical circuit. The dull ache in my upper jaw intensified, causing me to grit my teeth and clench my fists in agony. The murmur of far-off voices clarified into speech, synchronising with the thumping of two heartbeats—one frenetic, the other a calm counterpoint. Reality seeped back into my senses, as the burn within me dulled to embers.

"You need to eat," I heard the familiar British accent.

"I know," the croaky voice replied. "But I want to be here when she wakes up," the voice continued, and the other sighed.

"Very well, I'll bring a bag in." Their feet thudded against the hardwood floors.

"Nathaniel," the vampire replied in a hum. "Thank you for everything," the voice whispered. The door creaked open and closed once more. I took a deep breath, my lungs felt hollow, and the air was unnecessary. The air held an odd bouquet: familiar, yet mixed with something unsettling.

I shifted a little, my foot bumping into something furry. Atem. I couldn't help but smile when Atem trilled, and some of my motor functions came back.

"Hey," I heard the same voice whisper.

I opened my eyes a little, squinting to shield my eyes. Everything was so bright, clear, yet not a single ray of light was in the room. Is this what night vision is like?

This isn't my room.

Neil's dark grey eyes bore into mine. I frowned a little, feeling like I just got hit by a train, lit on fire, and getting over the flu at the same time. Shifting my weight, I nestled into the contours of Neil's bed, seeking comfort where I could find it.

"Hey yourself," I croaked and tried to clear it, but felt the horrible stabbing pain.

"Hungry?" he asked me. I thought about it for a second. Putting two and two together, the fiery burning pain throughout the body was also hunger.

Atem rubbed his head against my hand, demanding to be petted. I sniffed the air one more time and breathed a sigh of relief.

"Yeah," I murmured. Neil smiled, leaning closer to me, his lips touching my forehead. He tilted his head against mine and took a deep breath in. It was as if a flock of butterflies erupted in my stomach, and a phantom heartbeat kept pace with them. Shadows of old feelings crawled out from their hidden corners, emotions I'd tried to bury.

"I understand if you felt nothing," Neil breathed. "I treated you like shit when you were human," he pulled back, his grey eyes turning soft and warm. "If you can give me a chance, I'll make things right," he whispered. I shrugged at Neil, giving him a cheeky smile.

"Hmmm, I mean, I could forgive you," Neil smiled. "But I don't know, relationships just seem like a lot of work, and I have to give you attention, and Atem needs more love and..." I stopped myself, knowing the joke was over before it even started. He jumped on the bed, just missing Atem and lifting me off the bed and wrapping me into a hug. We stared at each other, enjoying the silence and comfort we brought. He brushed his fingers through my hair, putting the stray strands behind my ear.

"You are becoming the new definition of evil." He smiled. I took in his smile, the joy in his eyes. I loved seeing him like this, sincere, sweet, happy. Fallon wouldn't want it any other way for her son. I leaned forward, my lips touching his cheek. I took note that he no longer felt cold against my skin.

"I'm just teasing," I whispered. "Give it time, ok?" I asked him. Neil nodded and put his forehead to mine.

"Whether it be a hundred years or a thousand, I'll be patient, I'll be kind, I will wait till you feel the same. I am yours for eternity, my love," he whispered. My throat felt tight; I exhaled, releasing the breath I didn't know I was holding.

We both heard Nathaniel clear his throat. I turned to the older vampire, my eyebrow raised. His stache twitched with his mouth.

I took a deep breath, inhaling the sweet smell of roses. My body felt like someone had set a flame, and my eyes landed on the glass of blood in Nathaniel's hand. Red and oh so sweet. A dryness seized my mouth, and I felt a sharp elongation from my gums—fangs, craving the sight before me.

It felt as if my body wasn't my own.

The lukewarm blood splashed against my tongue, sweet but a little stale and not as warm as I hoped it would be. Trailing down my throat, dousing the fire and pooling into my stomach. My fangs ached, desperate to bite into tender flesh and hear the begging screams of my prey. I licked the glass clean. Snarling, I crushed the glass and shards scattered all over the floor.

"More." I snarled as a ravenous void gnawed at my insides.

"We'll get you more," Nathaniel sighed. He approached me with ease and was careful to take my hand in his. The cuts on my hand stitched themselves together.

"Shit, sorry Nathaniel," I apologised.

"It's fine," he assured and began picking up the shards of glass.

"I don't know what came over me!" My voice was shaking with hysteria.

"Just your nature, it happens to all newly turned. Your need for blood is uncontrolled." Neil came over and wrapped his arms around me in comfort.

"And when will I be?" I asked.

"Six months."

Oh god, that long, I don't have time! I have a job, uni, and my blog. It will be awhile before I can write anything, since the cat is out of the bag.

A few familiar faces stared at us through the open door of his room. I swallowed, remembering who these people are and realising they have witnessed my monstrous nature. I stood behind Neil, instincts telling me to stay close to my sire.

God, this is embarrassing.

“Whelp, she’s fine. I’m outta here,” I heard a familiar voice. Ceres sculled her drink and made a disgusted face.

“For a city that has become famous for being the coffee city of the nation, you sure have shitty instant,” she huffed and walked over to the kitchen.

“Ceres!” Bellamy hissed at her, and she gave him the bird.

“Told you it was crap,” I murmured to Nathaniel. He growled at me in response.

“Oh please,” she walked to the door frame, staring at Nathaniel and Neil. “Is this necessary, or is this some vampire thing I don’t understand?” she asked them both with her hands on her hips. I heard her heartbeat was slower than usual, by about half a second, which is not normal for a regular human. Her scent was quite peculiar, emitting a sweet fragrance but with an off-putting odour, almost like she has expired.

At least I won't try to eat her.

"You're a half-breed. Of course, you wouldn't understand," Bellamy answered for Neil and Nathaniel.

"Ok, before you trash our home," Brooklyn says as he stepped in between them. "She's fine, alive. You got to stick around and make sure, please leave."

"You came to check on me?" I asked, poking my head out.

Ceres smiled and shrugged a little. "I was there at the fight. I got worried." Ceres played it cool, and Bellamy rolled his eyes at her.

"We have a few things to discuss, but it can wait," Bellamy explained, getting up from the couch.

"Yes! Please do!" Brooklyn ran to the door and opened it for them. "We have a few things to discuss ourselves." Brooklyn looked at me, and I hid again. Feeling like a child who was about to have a talk with his father. The sound of departing footsteps and a door closing spoke louder than any goodbye. Neil growled a little as Brooklyn approached.

"Valeria," I heard his stern voice. I scuttled away from Neil and presented myself to Brooklyn, struggling to remain eye contact. The burly vampire had his arms crossed, his eyebrow raised.

"I-I," Words snagged in my throat, failing to form. Brooklyn wrapped me in a bear hug.

“I’m so glad you’re alive,” he says, breathed a sigh of relief.

“You’re not mad?” I asked him.

“Mad about the blog, yes. Happy to see you home, also yes.” Home. This is my home, my family. Brooklyn let me go and gave a slight nod. “We need to talk about that blog, though.”

'I guess you could say I’m banned? Or, at least until I change the names and identity of everyone or change my hosting provider. Apparently, there is someone who knows someone, and that someone knows another someone who develops servers for the supernatural. Social media, shopping, blood bags, blogs. Pretty cool. A lot of work. But it’s good to be home.'

Blog 40

Date: Dec 4th
Time: 9:15AM

'This will be my last post on the site. I plan to write more, but I need to create a safe place for my family. I can't let this happen again. Don't worry, though. I'll let you all know when it's happening. Instead of living with three vampires, it will be about me, living with normal, human roommates, original as it can get. Cliched, I know.

But being a vampire is weird. All of it is weird but natural at the same time. I'm looking into this way too much.'

The idea of goodbye weighed like a leaden anchor in my chest. Showered in so much love and support, the thought of it ending gnawed at me. Can I keep fuelling this fire, or will it eventually dwindle to ashes? Like a tv series, it can last only so long before the ideas run out. I dread for that to happen.

Doubts whirl in my mind, each one a claw grip tightening on my nerves. The room felt like a vacuum, devoid of any sound except for the relentless echo of my thoughts.

I felt two secure arms wrap around me, hair on my face.

"You're overthinking again," Neil murmurs.

"It's gonna be shit," I mumble, feeling a frantic energy skittering under my skin.

"It won't. If humans enjoyed your human life, turned vampires would enjoy your newly turned vampire life. They may need something like this. It might relate to a lot of them," Neil assures and kisses me on the cheek.

"Yeah, a place where we all complain about our hunger, how we still do human-like things, and how annoying our sires can be," I tease, a wry smile gracing my lips.

"Hey, I'm not that annoying," Neil defends, and I laugh.

"Says the person who is slothing over me while I work and whines whenever I give Atem too much attention," I argue, giving my evidence.

"Only cause you love the cat more than me," Neil retorts, his lower lip jutting out in a faux pout.

"I am–rather–very fond of you," I smile, leaning my head against his.

"Did you quote that movie?" His voice was muffled as he spoke.

"Yeah, but it describes the situation."

Neil chuckles and removes his head from my shoulder. I lift my head out of the way and feel his lips touch my cheek. I smile, turning to look at him, letting our lips touch.

I wouldn't have this any other way. This is my life now, my home, my family.

End

Ten Chapter Special!

Why?

Timeline: Before Blog 5

Valeria lay sprawled on the shaggy rug, clutching a worn-out book to her chest. Her eyes shimmered, and a dreamy smile graced her lips as she lost herself in the unfolding love story. Each time the characters professed their love for each other, her heart skipped a beat, imagining herself and her literary crush—her Senpai—in their places.

"So, when are you going to this concert?" Brooklyn's voice cut through her reverie as he rustled around in the kitchen.

Holding a bag of cold blood, he cringed as he selected a mug from the cabinet—Nathaniel's fine china. The memory of a chaotic day on the garden balcony washed over him. He shook his head. Fine china was meant for tea, not for blood. He decanted the blood into a dull blue mug and tossed the empty bag into the trash.

"Next weekend. Senpai will be there," Valeria sighed, pulling herself up to a sitting position. Her heart still rode the highs of her daydreams, evident in the lingering smile on her face.

"Uh-huh," Brooklyn responded, eyebrows raised. "You're sure he's going to be there?"

“His favourite band is playing. Besides, I like the band too,” she defended, brushing her hair away from her eyes.

Neil, also known as Lord Brooding, was sitting alone in his room, browsing through social media posts about the man Valeria was infatuated with. Each photo, each comment, stoked the embers of his growing resentment.

"Why does she even like this guy?" Neil snarled under his breath, glaring at his phone. At first, his impulse had been to sabotage Valeria's life, maybe even kill her. But something within him had shifted. His vampiric instincts whispered, nagged at him, their urgings growing more strident with each passing day. It's rare for them to split, and become separate entity. Starvation, or when something is incorrect, and the thinking mind does not listen to nature's subtle hints are the only moment they act out. He had tried to ignore them, but the disquiet had grown impossible to shake off.

"Why exactly do you like this human?" Brooklyn's voice, slightly muffled, carried into Neil's room.

“It’s a combination of things,” Valeria replied. “One, I admire him as an author, and I wish for something similar–loyal readers and surviving off the books I create–that’s why he’s Senpai. I want to learn from him. Two, I like his face. It’s a pleasant face to look at.”

Neil felt something snap within him. He agreed with Brooklyn; Valeria didn't even know this guy.

"What if he's just a massive playboy?" Brooklyn pressed Valeria. "What then?"

Her face clouded. "Then my illusion shatters, and that would be disappointing, wouldn't it? That's the risk you take idolizing someone."

Neil sat up, intrigued despite himself. Though he didn't fully understand why, the idea of disrupting this fantasy of Valeria's brought a newfound sense of purpose. It was as if a new strategy had unfolded before him, lifting the weight of the last twenty aimless years from his shoulders.

Muddled thoughts

Before Blog 6

Neil had been prepared to execute his plan, but something had shifted in him. After a week of living with them, he found he no longer despised her. In fact, he discovered an unexpected comfort in her quiet presence, how she patiently sat through Nathaniel's long-winded monologues without batting an eye. Her initial shyness had melted away with each passing week, and she seemed to be finding her place in their odd household. No longer a wallflower or an object that was just a part of the furniture.

He can recount one evening, Valeria, believing herself to be alone, headphones on, blasting Short Stack and dancing like an idiot in the kitchen. Neil watched from a doorway as she danced around, blocking out the world.

Neil admired how carefree she was then, loving the present moment, dancing out whatever scene was in her head. Her lips moved, mumbling dialogue between fictional characters, which she would pause to scribble down. While others might find her behaviour peculiar, it captivated Neil; it was a quirk he enjoyed listening to. He could practically see the gears turning in her head, her mind a complex tapestry of plots and characters. A part of Neil grew excited, thinking about showing her the other worlds and watching her mind wander with possibilities for a story. Her imagination would go insane.

But he also saw the other side of her. The days when she became a silent shell, avoiding the things she loved, scrolling through social media as if looking for something that eluded her grasp. On those days, he found himself pushing her buttons, provoking any reaction just to break the stillness that hung around her. Anger, he figured, was better than apathy.

“I still don’t understand why you tagged along,” Valeria's voice broke through his thoughts as they walked through Melbourne's eerily quiet streets in the early morning.

He toyed with the truth—To kill your Senpai—but bit it back. "To make your life a misery, remember?" he said instead, although he knew he no longer wished that upon her.

She yawned, her voice cracking with fatigue. “Uh-huh. Well, when you come up with something more original, let me know.”

Neil noticed her discomfort, her throat parched. They passed a corner store still open at this late hour—a far cry from the restricted hours of his 1970s past. Pulling her inside, he ignored her protests. They were alone except for another man, clad entirely in black, eyeing Neil with recognition and malice.

Neil felt his fingers elongate into deadly claws, ready for the inevitable. Valeria bumped into him, finally catching onto the tension.

"Hold it!" She stepped between them, eyes flashing with frustration. "Do we have to do this now? I want to go home. I'm tired and not in the mood for whatever this is."

Their faces registered surprise, then reluctance. The hunter backed off, paid for his items, and left, eyeing Neil.

Amused and impressed, Neil turned back to his original mission—a bottle of water. He grabbed one and headed for the checkout. Once the transaction was complete, he handed the bottle to a perplexed Valeria.

She hesitated for a moment before taking it. "Thank you," she finally said, the words tinged with a new understanding, perhaps a fragile beginning. And for the first time, Neil felt he might be ready to understand it, too.

Paranoid

After blog 13

Neil's obsession has become a little unhealthy. His fists clench every time he saw Valeria walk alone at night. He loathes himself for following her, but he reminds himself that he doesn't watch her sleep like that creep from the movie.

Neil told himself that it was only about self-preservation; she was his prey, after all. But deep down, he knew he was lying to himself. As he lurked in the shadows, his eyes would follow her retreating figure, and his heart would inexplicably tighten each time she turned a corner, disappearing from his line of sight.

He had killed countless predators who had dared to threaten her, but he couldn't explain why he was so hell-bent on protecting this human. After all, he'd lost his appetite for life decades ago. Food had become nothing more than a necessity, stripping his meals back to once a week. Yet, he couldn't bring himself to end his existence.

A booming voice pulled him out of his thoughts. "Out of the stories I have heard about you, people watching was never your thing."

Before he knew it, Neil found himself yanked from his hidden spot and tossed deeper into the dark alley. The vampire who had spoken, a burly creature twice Neil's size, stood before him, smirking. A gang of sneering vampires circled around them. Neil picked himself up, brushing the dirt off his skinny jeans.

"What do you want?" Neil spat out, his eyes pointed.

The large vampire chuckled, "When I heard you were following a human and protecting them, I had to see it for myself. Since when did you care about anything?"

Neil sidestepped the question. "Since when did you care about my existence?"

The burly vampire laughed, flashing his fangs. "You're the only vampire that I know who hates everything. I wanted to know what's so special about this human."

Neil moved closer, making the vampires flinch in anticipation. He sauntered past their leader, shrugging dismissively. "She's just a human, I've claimed. If you want her, she's all yours."

The leader growled, sceptical. "You've never been one to draw out the hunt."

"Who says I can't change? Sometimes it's fun to get close, then crush them from the inside," Neil lied, maintaining his facade of indifference.

The burly vampire still looked unconvinced. "Don't attract more hunters," he snarled, finally relenting. A gust of wind blew, and suddenly Neil was alone in the alley again.

Who cares if it does? Neil thought bitterly, staring after the retreating vampires. In the end, we're all bound for the same fate.

But as he stepped out of the alley, resuming his watch over Valeria from a distance, he couldn't shake the feeling that maybe, just maybe, they could change some fates.

I kicked my roommates out for you – please like me.

After Blog 3

Frustrated, Nathaniel flung Valeria's scattered clothes into a laundry basket and scraped crusted food off plates, dumping them into the sink. The scent of human food made Nathaniel wrinkle his nose and reminded him of a night he would rather forget - a grand banquet where he was forced to eat. He had later thrown it all up, his body rebelling against the alien sustenance. A shudder ran through him, disrupting the memory.

Brooklyn's laughter from that night echoed in his mind, and Nathaniel clenched his fists. Shaking off the humiliating memory, he continued his frantic cleaning.

Fumbling with the remote, he muttered curses at Neil for even suggesting they install the problematic projector screen. Just as he finally managed to retract it into the ceiling, a knock echoed through the still-messy apartment.

His pulse, if he had one, would've skyrocketed. An advisor to the king was coming, and this was his chance to gain some much-needed recognition within the coven. Drawing a deep, unnecessary breath to calm himself, Nathaniel rushed to the door and opened it.

Two oddly dressed vampires greeted him. One sported long, curly brown hair and wore what Nathaniel could only describe as a fashion abomination—long sweatpants and a loose cotton shirt. The other's hair was shorter but equally unkempt, and his black hoodie clashed with a red shirt and skinny jeans. Nathaniel questioned his decision-making; had he invited complete strangers by accident?

Nervous but attempting to appear composed, Nathaniel ushered them in. "Bellamy and Jayson, I presume?"

They grinned, revealing their fangs. "That's us."

Jayson sniffed the air as he entered, and Nathaniel cringed inwardly. "May I offer you two a drink?"

Jayson's eyes dulled to a dark grey as he nodded. Meanwhile, Bellamy had walked over to the balcony door. "What a lovely garden. Do you tend to it, Nathaniel?"

"No, that would be my roommate Brooklyn," Nathaniel replied, his hands trembling slightly as he tore open a packet of blood. He couldn't afford to mess this up.

Jayson interrupted his thoughts. "Is he the human?"

"No, he's one of us," Nathaniel quickly replied, grateful for the microwave's beep signalling the heated blood was ready. "He just has an odd fondness for gardening."

"Strange, I was hoping to meet your roommates," Bellamy chimed in.

Nathaniel's hands almost fumbled with the hot porcelain. "Brooklyn isn't a fan of politics, and Neil hates—"

"Wait. Neil?" Bellamy cut in.

"If it's the same, Neil, I thought he was long dead," Bellamy said, trailing off into silence. Nathaniel's mind froze, grasping at Bellamy's implication.

Jayson broke the silence by grabbing the glass of warmed blood. "Then who's the human?"

"An experiment Neil undertook," Nathaniel replied tersely, his frustration mounting. "She answered an ad and now lives with us."

The two vampires exchanged a knowing glance. "Interesting," Bellamy finally said. “Let's talk business, shall we?”

Glad to shift the focus, Nathaniel led them to the couches. The night promised to be a long one, indeed.

Two Weeks Later

Nathaniel tore open an envelope marked 'URGENT' from his bank. He unfolded the enclosed statement and his eyes widened in disbelief. "Brooklyn!" he bellowed, his voice thick with outrage. "You spent twenty-five thousand? Just for one room?!"

Is Revenge Best Served Hot or Cold?

After Blog 3

Valeria collected stray belongings from around her room, tucking them into her duffle bag with more force than needed. Each item seemed to echo the finality of her decision. Her eyes brimmed with unshed tears, her heart a raw wound in her chest.

Neil and Brooklyn, stationed near the front door, watched in a flurry of their frantic friend clean up the place. Brooklyn folded his arms, shooting a disapproving glare at the posh vampire for snapping at the young human. Neil seemed as indifferent as ever. Yet Brooklyn sensed an undercurrent of tension and held his tongue, waiting for the right moment to unleash his thoughts.

As Valeria stepped out of her room, her eyes met Nathaniel's. Meanwhile, Neil and Brooklyn leaned against the doorframe, hands idly in their pockets. Something about their stance struck her as off, but she couldn't put her finger on it. Brushing past them without a word, she opened the door and stepped into the lit hallway that led to the elevator.

Neil and Brooklyn followed her, closing the door behind them and leaving Nathaniel to his cleanup.

"So, where do you plan to go?" Brooklyn broke the silence.

Valeria shrugged, her gaze dropping to the rug beneath her feet. Neil felt a twinge in his gut, a dull ache amplifying by the second. He clenched his jaw, suppressing the surge of protective anger that welled up inside him.

“In a hostel somewhere. Few places are cheap,” Valeria muttered.

Brooklyn's face contorted, lips puckering as if he'd just tasted something sour. Exchanging a glance with Neil, he took a step back, ensuring their conversation remained private.

“She's strapped for cash,” Neil whispered.

“And here I thought she was doing fine,” Brooklyn whispered back, both men watching Valeria, who remained oblivious, her attention still focused on the nondescript carpet.

“No, times are tough. Even basic groceries are expensive," Neil muttered, a brief flash of a recent grocery bill crossing his mind.

Brooklyn grinned, a devilish upturn of his lips. “So that's why you've been buying her food.”

Before he could second guess himself, Neil landed a punch on Brooklyn's shoulder. While ineffective, it proved immensely satisfying.

"Look, she's struggling to find work, okay? Just leave it at that," Neil snapped before stalking off.

As the elevator arrived and its doors opened, Brooklyn grinned at Neil and Valeria. "Wanna get revenge?" he teased, waving a silver card before them. Their faces lit up in response.

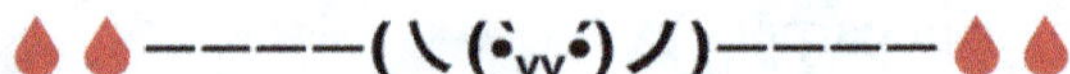

Valeria was the last to exit the yellow taxi. As they entered the hotel lobby, she felt the weight of eyes on her, scrutinizing her every move.

Brooklyn sauntered in first, barefoot yet brimming with confidence. Neil followed at a measured pace, while Valeria lagged behind, wishing she could disappear into her own skin.

As Brooklyn handled the booking, Neil took notice of Valeria's defensive posture: her grip tightened on her duffle bag, her eyes flicking nervously around the entrance.

“Guess which room I got?” Brooklyn's voice cut through the tension.

“The closest one?” Neil guessed.

“No,” Brooklyn sighed, rolling his eyes. “We're in the Villa. And I've arranged for massages, wine, a buffet dinner, and breakfast. All for you.” he handed Valeria a key card.

Valeria felt her heart swell, her eyes misting over. She took a shuddering breath, releasing some of the tension she had held onto for so long. Brooklyn, initially alarmed, relaxed when Valeria shook her head and chuckled.

“I'm just overwhelmed. Thank you, I didn’t expect this,” she said, wiping away a tear.

Inside the opulent hotel restaurant, Valeria couldn't help but marvel at the lavish spread before her. Her eyes darted from the sushi to the steaks, her mouth watering at the sight of the dessert bar.

Neil watched her, his eyes taking on a predatory glint. He found himself drawn to her vulnerability, her sheer joy at the simplest of pleasures.

Brooklyn sidled up to Neil. "How's guard duty going?" he whispered, chuckling at Neil's discomfort.

“Don't know what you're talking about,” Neil retorted.

“Sure, you don't,” Brooklyn smirked. “You wouldn’t go to all this trouble for just any human.”

“Just playing a game,” Neil hissed, but Brooklyn isn’t buying it. “I’m gonna–I’m gonna,” Neil cuts himself off, and Brooklyn is about to burst out laughing but is trying to hold it in. “I don’t have to explain myself to you,” Neil snarls at the older vampire and storms off. Brooklyn waves Neil goodbye and shook his head, amused. He turned his attention back to Valeria, who was piling her plate high with food. Around them, the well-heeled guests crinkled their noses in distaste.

Brooklyn snarled softly under his breath. Tonight, he'd be damned if anyone dared to ruin her moment.

Nap Time

Deleted Chapter

Nathaniel stared at his favourite shaggy rug, now transformed into a bed for Valeria. She lay there clad in a fuzzy suit resembling a purple dinosaur—or was it a dragon? With its hood and horned tail, the costume mystified him. A heavy sigh escaped his lips as he gingerly stepped over her, careful not to awaken the human slumbering so inconveniently on the floor.

Just as he lifted one foot over Valeria, the oak door behind him creaked open. Nathaniel froze and twisted his torso to shush Neil, who had just entered the room.

Neil paused, his eyes narrowing at the sight before him. Nathaniel, caught stepping over Valeria, appeared to be in a precarious position—a position that made Neil's blood simmer with irritation.

"Shh!" Nathaniel's eyes widened, darting toward Valeria as if fearing her sudden awakening. Neil observed this, his moustache quivering in what could only be anticipation.

Neil took a moment to scan his gaze over Valeria, stretched out on the floor. Dressed in her usual nerdy attire, completely unaware of the fuss she was causing.

As if on cue, the sound of humming approached the glass door. Both Nathaniel and Neil tensed, their eyes locking onto Brooklyn, who entered with a slide so forceful the entire city of Melbourne might have heard it.

"Shh!" they both admonished in hushed voices, causing Brooklyn to halt and look between them in puzzlement.

Brooklyn noticed Nathaniel's odd stance—arms elevated as though navigating a balance beam—and Neil's intense gaze locked on Nathaniel's precarious footwork. Despite the obstructed view behind the couch, he discerned Valeria's purple, fuzzy form sprawled on the rug. A grin slowly crept across Brooklyn's face.

"She's always like this," Nathaniel whispered, his voice tinged with exasperation.

"Then why haven't you moved?" Neil hissed in reply, earning himself another "shush" from Nathaniel.

Just then, Valeria stirred, turning onto her side. Nathaniel's body stiffened, his breath caught in his throat. A sigh of relief escaped his lips when he realised she remained asleep.

"I don't want to wake her," he finally growled, resuming his careful stepping over Valeria. No sooner had he felt relief wash over him than his foot caught on the tail of her costume, sending him sprawling face-first onto the rug.

Neil shook his head incredulously while suppressing a chuckle, watching as Valeria scrunched her face in reaction to Nathaniel's theatrical fall. She then stretched lazily and went back to sleep.

Unable to contain his amusement, Brooklyn dashed to the balcony and released peals of laughter into the night air. Composing himself, he returned to the room where Nathaniel was now meticulously brushing off his suit.

"Should we move her?" Brooklyn whispered.

Neil, now seated on the couch next to Valeria, shook his head. "I'll keep an eye on her. We don't need another spectacle from Nathaniel."

Brooklyn held up ten fingers, struggling to contain another burst of laughter. "That's ten trips so far."

Nathaniel snorted dismissively. "Well, if she'd sleep somewhere more appropriate, this wouldn't happen."

As the roommates began discussing designated sleeping zones for Valeria, they came to a begrudging agreement. Nathaniel finally conceded, albeit reluctantly, "Fine. She can stay here—as long as she doesn't ruin the rug."

With that, Nathaniel stormed upstairs, leaving Neil and Brooklyn to finalise the sleeping arrangements.

Brooklyn returned to the balcony while Neil reclined on the couch. His eyes met Valeria's briefly as she stirred, giving him a sleepy smile before drifting back into slumber. Neil relaxed, comforted by the rhythmic sound of her heartbeat as he, too, drifted into a peaceful sleep.

Oh shit

During Blog 14

Neil crouched in the shadows across the narrow, bustling street. He watched the human girl—Valeria—glance anxiously from her phone to the street and back again. She looked left, then right, as if expecting someone or something.

He clenched his fists, irritation darkening his features. Why had he followed her here? Why should he care that she was waiting for a date?

Over the past five months, he'd observed her becoming a fixture in their home and noticed his roommates growing genuinely fond of her. It irked him, the way they fussed over her, as if her human fragility made her special. His resentment toward his roommates only deepened.

Yet, he couldn't ignore his own contradictions. He found himself ensuring she arrived home safely or covertly mentioning her financial difficulties to Brooklyn and Nathaniel, who'd inevitably step in to help. Even his own lifestyle had shifted; the nights of reckless encounters were behind him. Brooklyn said he'd changed for the better, and Neil hated that he might be right. Emotional attachment was a vulnerability he couldn't afford.

His hand dug into the brick wall behind him, knuckles white, as flashes of past pain and loss coursed through him. He felt like his chest was splitting open. Eyes closed, he focused on his breath, willing the agony to subside. When he opened his eyes and released the wall, fragments of brick tumbled down, clattering to the ground.

Time for a drink, he thought, moving further into the darkness. The underground bar—exclusive to vampires—was nearby.

The place was as he remembered it: dark, loud, suffused with the smell of sweat and the intoxicating aroma of humans. His mouth watered at the scent. He considered throwing caution to the wind, but stopped himself. He'd been thrown out before and didn't want a repeat performance.

All Neil wants is a cold beer, a dark corner and some bimbo to come over and tell him how pretty he is– just enough to stroke his ego and make himself feel better.

Slipping into a shadowy corner, he sipped his cold beer. No one approached him, and Neil's mind turned inwards, brooding over why Valeria would prefer her date over him. Neil absently cracks the glass in his grip.

They could be holding hands. Another crack.

They could be laughing, joking, enjoying each other's company. The same crack grows bigger.

Sitting together, side by side. Another crack fissures.

I bet he chose a horror movie. More cracks form, creating intricate designs in the glass.

Then they kiss. Neil's thoughts swept away to the back of his head as his hand soaked in beer, rushing over the counter like a tsunami and drenched his clothes.

The bartender barks out to him and rushes over to the mess Neil had created.

"Sorry, sorry," Neil grumbles, shaking his wet hand in the air. The bartender uses an old tea towel.

“You're cut off,” the bartender barked, cleaning the mess.

A familiar voice interrupted Neil's internal cursing. "I thought I told you not to come here ever again," said Limbani, the club's owner.

“Hello, Limbani,” he drawls. Putting his hands up like the police have caught him.

Limbani crosses her arms and gives Neil a hard stare. Upturning her plump lips and baring her fangs at him.

“You think you can walk in here, after the mess you caused me all those years ago?” she snaps, marching towards the white vampire, hissing in his face. “I had to lie low because of those hunters. I lost business because of you!”

Neil could only roll his eyes in response, much to Limbani's displeasure, and she snatches the hairs at the back of his head. Neil gasps in agony as the sharp pain travels through his skull.

"I get, I get, I'm sorry," Neil cracks. Limbani lets go, and Neil can feel the relief and rub the back of his head.

"Leave." She snarls, turning away from him.

"Look." Neil breathes. Limbani stops in her tracks. "I just want a drink. Be alone and go home. I don't want any trouble." Limbani was in his face again, grasping Neil by the throat and lifting him off the ground.

"Don't want trouble? Maybe you should have thought of that before you ruined my club." Neil can feel her claws digging into his throat. "Slaughtering a small group of humans."

“You joined in,” Neil rasps.

“You left a trail,” Limbani throws Neil across the room and landing against a brick wall. Some debris of brick falls on top of his head.

Neil looks up and sees Limbani’s coven stand by her side, their arms crossed, fangs on display. “Throw him out with the rest of the trash,” she snarls, walking away.

They hoisted Neil from the ground. He had a chance to fight back or stand up for himself as two of Limbani’s brutes tossed him out to the street, lucky to miss the puddle of water.

Just a little over ten years ago, Neil was tossed out the same way.

Arriving home, Neil felt defeated: tired, sore, sober. And then he saw her. Valeria perched on

Nathaniel's coffee table, sniffling. Anger flared inside him; he wanted to find the man responsible for her tears.

"Hey," is all Neil croaks and put his jacket away.

Neil is beside Valeria, now both sitting on Nathaniel's coffee table. "How was the date?" Neil before kicking himself for asking such a stupid question. *'how was the date?' Neil, you can see what has happened.*

He listened as she spilled her woes, her disappointments. He interrupted her lament to point out the aspects of her that were uniquely her, things he had come to appreciate. The fragile smile she offered broke something inside him.

As Valeria retreated to her room, Neil was left alone with the newfound revelation pounding in his skull. *I love her.*

His body trembled uncontrollably, past promises never to form emotional bonds resounding in his head. Memories of loved ones lost overwhelmed him, his chest tightening unbearably. He collapsed to the floor, trembling, suddenly aware that he'd walled off his grief for too long. He thought of all he'd lost and realised he'd been running away, using the thrill of the hunt, booze, and meaningless connections as crutches.

Lying there, racked with tremors of emotional agony, Neil finally understood the risk of loving again. It was the risk of exposing old wounds, of enduring new heartache. But as he shook, a single, desperate thought pierced through his anguish: Make this stop.

Nip it in the bud before the bud nips me

During Blog 16

Neil waited as Nathaniel ushered Brooklyn in from the garden balcony. His leg bounced nervously, arms crossed over his chest. The lingering scent of the dog from their recent garden visit filled his nostrils.

His eyes snapped shut, as if he could imprison his memories in a vault deep within him. Unidentifiable emotions churned, threatening to break free. He had built walls—high and unyielding—that kept his friends, or rather roommates, at a safe distance. But now, those walls felt like they were closing in on him.

Regret surged through him as he thought of his behaviour toward Nathaniel and Brooklyn, who had put up with his icy demeanour and uncontrollable bloodlust.

His fists clenched and his teeth ground together, as if he could physically suppress the turmoil inside him.

The lump in his throat refused to dissipate. Salty tears threatened to spill over as memories of his old family, his mother, overwhelmed him.

"Neil?"

His head shot up, eyes flinging open to meet the concerned gazes of the vampires before him. His breathing evened and his fangs retracted. For now, he managed to cap his swirling emotions, but he wasn't sure how long that would last.

"I'm fine!" he snapped, looking away from their probing eyes.

"Very well," Nathaniel said, clearing his throat.

It's all her fault, Neil snarled inwardly. If she hadn't appeared, he wouldn't have fallen in love, wouldn't have cared, wouldn't have had to confront anything.

"She has no one." Nathaniel's words broke through Neil's reverie.

A twisted smile tugged at his lips. Here was a solution, an answer to his silent prayers. No one would notice if she disappeared; no one would care. He could kill her, repair everything, and forget. Love wouldn't be an issue.

But you'll be lonely again, his inner voice warned him, as it often did when he was conflicted.

All eyes turned to the front door as Valeria shuffled in, her feet barely crossing the threshold. Neil sprang to his feet, feeling his fangs lengthen. Brooklyn lunged, attempting to grab Neil, but Neil's speed outmatched him.

Leaping over the furniture, Neil pinned Valeria to the floor, his fangs hovering over her throat. His better nature screamed at him to stop, but he silenced it, resolute in his twisted mission.

Fear can make people do foolish and cruel things.

"I told you I would kill someday." Outwardly, Neil seemed heartless, but inwardly, nausea churned as he sank his fangs into her flesh.

💧💧-----(ヽ(•̀vv•́)ノ)-----💧💧

Afterward, everything became a haze for Neil. Flashes of Valeria's sweet blood, sharp pain in his spine from Brooklyn's counterattack, and finally being thrown back into the apartment. When he next opened his eyes, he was alone in his room.

He stumbled out of bed, feeling his vertebrae realign, and his limbs regain function. Crawling partway across the white carpet, he finally managed to stand.

Neil opened the door to find his two roommates waiting for him, arms crossed, fangs bared.

"Well, shit," he thought.

"Sit," Brooklyn commanded.

Neil shuffled out of his room and sat in the armchair, his roommates looming over him, their expressions foreboding.

Here we go again.

A Fated Night

After Blog 34–Backstory

They thrust Nathaniel onto the streets, landing face-first into a puddle as if it had been waiting just for him. Laughter erupted from the vampires, who tossed his hat and gloves after him.

"Go back to your motherland, you posh poof!" they jeered. With a grimace, Nathaniel lifted himself from the puddle, his clothes sullied.

Brooklyn emerged from the club, his hands buried in his jean pockets. Seeing his fallen friend, he extended a hand and offered a sad smile. Nathaniel grunted but seized the offered hand, rising to his feet.

Nathaniel sighed, his eyes scanning the damage to his meticulously pressed suit. His jacket had suffered the most, but his shirt was soaked through. As his fingers brushed over the fabric, he took a moment to be thankful that his face remained unmarred.

Too pretty for scars.

Each act of humiliation stung, each rejection from the upper classes making his lofty ambitions seem ever more unattainable. Brooklyn remained his only constant.

Appreciation for Brooklyn filled Nathaniel. The man's steady support had been a pillar. He leaned on time and again. He marvelled at how Brooklyn, a loner by nature with a passion for plants and a disdain for vampire politics, remained by his side.

"Are you all right?" Brooklyn asked, giving Nathaniel's shoulder a reassuring slap. Nathaniel swallowed hard, holding back tears.

"I am fine, just a setback is all," he said, brushing Brooklyn's hand off his shoulder. With a flourish, he added, "I'll have them eating out of my palm in no time! I just need to go from a different angle."

Brooklyn chuckled at Nathaniel's grandiosity. "Well, first, let's get you into some dry clothes. You wanna look your best."

Sheepishly, Nathaniel let his hands fall to his sides. "Ah yes, fair point," he agreed, flashing Brooklyn a grateful smile. "What would I ever do without you, my friend?"

"In a gutter with no shoulder to cry on?" Brooklyn quipped. Both laughed as Nathaniel playfully slapped Brooklyn's back.

As they ambled toward home, playful banter filled the air. They had turned insult-throwing into a sort of game, it would doom the loser of which to a month of apartment cleaning.

Suddenly, Nathaniel halted outside a dimly lit alley, his nostrils flaring at the putrid scent of dog. Brooklyn noticed the abrupt stop and turned, grinning. "What? Did I win?"

Ignoring him, Nathaniel peered into the alley, his ears picking up faint, pained moans. Ignoring the instinctual warnings flaring within him, he ventured into the dark space between the buildings. "Nathaniel?" Brooklyn's voice echoed from the mouth of the alley. Nathaniel whipped his head around, baring his fangs in a silencing gesture.

Undeterred, Nathaniel continued on, Brooklyn's footsteps pounding as he caught up. Both men stopped dead in their tracks at the gruesome sight before them: a disfigured figure lay sprawled on the ground, limbs severed, organs exposed. The creature's head still attached, and heart still intact. A vampire. One of their own. The vampire before them stares at them. His mouth opened a little, noticing one fang is torn out of his mouth.

Brooklyn let out a horrified breath. "Oh god."

It’s ok to cry

Before Blog 39

A day had passed since Valeria suffered a werewolf attack, and Neil sat vigil beside her. His leg bounced in nervous anticipation; his eyes remained fixed on her unmoving form, willing her to wake up.

Three days. That's how long it took for a human to transition into a vampire. Blood would rewrite their cellular structure, halt the aging process, and reset the chemistry of the brain. A gnawing hunger would become the new baseline, flaring into fiery pain when ignored. The scientific explanation was relatively recent, but it did little to comfort Neil, whose understanding of the process remained marred by uncertainty.

The door creaked open, but Neil’s eyes didn't stray from Valeria. He felt a steadying hand grip his shoulder.

"You need to feed," Brooklyn's gravelly voice murmured into his ear.

"I'm fine," Neil rasped. His throat felt like it was ablaze, his nerves firing sharp stabs of pain through his body, urging him to feed.

"You're not. I'll sit with her till you get back," Brooklyn offered.

Neil's gaze stayed glued to Valeria. He could almost feel her eyes flicker open, hear her speak, feel her touch once again.

"I could have lost her," he whispered, his voice tinged with raw vulnerability as his eyes started to glisten. "She could have died in my arms."

Brooklyn looked at Neil, taken aback by the emotional display. He had waited for Neil to reconnect with this softer, more vulnerable side—a side kept only for their kin.

"It’s okay, we’re all here," Brooklyn said softly.

Neil shook his head, wiping away his tears, only for more to take their place. "No, it's not. I've treated you all terribly, distancing myself, thinking if I stopped caring, the pain would go, that I'd be invulnerable."

Brooklyn felt Neil tremble under his touch. He glanced up to see Nathaniel at the doorway, mouth open in disbelief. Ignoring Nathaniel's incredulous look, Brooklyn pulled Neil into a hug. Nathaniel joined in, completing the circle.

"I lost my family so long ago; I can't lose another. I’m so sorry, to all of you," Neil's voice broke as he clung to his friends.

Apologies couldn’t erase years of destructive behaviour, but they marked a beginning. Neil needed to let out years of pent-up emotion, to be told that it was okay to feel, to love, to be vulnerable.

"I’m so sorry," Neil whispered, tears still streaming down his face. "You're my brothers. I can't lose you. I can't lose anyone ever again."

Nathaniel and Brooklyn could only speculate about Neil’s past, likely filled with the tragic loss of a former coven. Vampires form unbreakable bonds. They might have their spats, but they would die for each other. The loss of a mate was the most devastating of all. Neil had Valeria, and losing her would mean losing himself.

"We're here for you," Brooklyn whispered back.

"Our family," Nathaniel added, causing Neil to sob even louder.

"I promise, I'll make things right," Neil wept, holding them tight, no intention of ever letting go.

Thank you.

From the Author

Thank you so much for your continued support and for buying a copy of my book. It was such a pleasure to write and write to you all. Receiving so many positive comments and love online only re-ignited my love for writing, reminding me why I started this.

I look forward to creating more stories for you all in the future. Keep an eye out online for future updates and stories!

Sunset

"What defines a monster? Is it their appearance – sharp teeth, eerie eyes, or rough skin? Or is it their actions, habits, and behaviour?"

These questions are explored as we journey to Ancient Rome where the head sorcerer makes a gruesome sacrifice in search of a particular soul. Syrus Valerius is the sole survivor, and he becomes the target of the people's ire. Alexandros takes Syrus under his wing, and a young girl named Annabeth soon enters his life. Despite facing adversity and prejudice, Syrus grows into adulthood and continues to fight against the harsh words of the people. However, as his 21st birthday approaches, he fears that all his efforts may be in vain.

Sunrise

Rune has lost all hope and is ready to embrace death after living on the streets for years. But when he is approached by Syrus Valerius, a vampire who has wandered the earth for centuries, he is offered eternal life. As a new vampire, Rune struggles to control his thirst for human blood and adapt to his new home. He must also navigate the complex dynamics of his relationship with Syrus.

However, Rune's troubled past resurfaces and threatens their newfound peace. In order to protect themselves, they must rely on the help of others and continue to learn and grow. Will they be able to overcome their past and secure their future together?

www.ingramcontent.com/pod-product-compliance
Lightning Source LLC
Chambersburg PA
CBHW060621310726
48982CB00003B/630

* 9 7 8 0 9 9 4 3 5 0 0 8 4 *